MOB HIT, RUSSIAN STYLE

A long black sedan pulled up to the curb a few feet from the two men on the corner. Both back doors of the vehicle opened, and two men exited from each side. As dim as the light from the streetlamp was, it cast enough illumination to kick a reflection off the gleaming metal barrels of the weapons they carried.

The big man saw them coming and dropped his cigar. The smaller man reached into his pocket and withdrew a revolver.

"Good God!" Olga muttered.

Vaughn pushed us into a doorway strewn with empty bottles and other trash.

We'd no sooner wedged into the cramped space when another automobile roared up, windows down, men hanging out holding automatic weapons. The firing erupted like a tornado, guns going off, men yelling, bullets ricocheting off the concrete above our heads. . . .

MURDER IN MOSCOW

A *Murder, She Wrote* Mystery

A Novel by Jessica Fletcher
and Donald Bain
based on the
Universal television series
created by Peter S. Fischer,
Richard Levinson & William Link

ⓞ
A SIGNET BOOK

SIGNET
Published by New American Library, a division of
Penguin Group (USA) Inc., 375 Hudson Street,
New York, New York 10014, USA
Penguin Group (Canada), 90 Eglinton Avenue East, Suite 700, Toronto,
Ontario M4P 2Y3, Canada (a division of Pearson Penguin Canada Inc.)
Penguin Books Ltd., 80 Strand, London WC2R 0RL, England
Penguin Ireland, 25 St. Stephen's Green, Dublin 2,
Ireland (a division of Penguin Books Ltd.)
Penguin Group (Australia), 250 Camberwell Road, Camberwell, Victoria 3124,
Australia (a division of Pearson Australia Group Pty. Ltd.)
Penguin Books India Pvt. Ltd., 11 Community Centre, Panchsheel Park,
New Delhi - 110 017, India
Penguin Group (NZ), 67 Apollo Drive, Rosedale, North Shore 0632,
New Zealand (a division of Pearson New Zealand Ltd.)
Penguin Books (South Africa) (Pty.) Ltd., 24 Sturdee Avenue,
Rosebank, Johannesburg 2196, South Africa

Penguin Books Ltd., Registered Offices:
80 Strand, London WC2R 0RL, England

First published by Signet, an imprint of New American Library,
a division of Penguin Group (USA) Inc.

First Printing, May 1998
20 19 18 17 16 15 14 13 12

For Marge and Emlyn
with love

Chapter One

"No, no, no, Mrs. Fletcher. It is pronounced *shch*, as in 'fresh cheese.' You run it together, Fre-*shch*-eese."

"I'm afraid I'm not doing very well," I said, slumping in my chair. "I never realized speaking Russian would be so difficult."

Professor Donskoy smiled. "I admire you wanting to learn to speak some Russian," he said, "but I'm sure those with whom you're meeting will speak English."

I sat forward. "But I want to show my respect by at least knowing a few basic phrases."

"Of course. People always respond favorably when a foreigner is interested enough to learn their language. But it can sometimes get you in trouble."

"How so?"

"Once you use a few of their words, they expect you to know much more. Better to be honest and say you speak only English."

"You may be right, Professor, but I'd still like to keep trying. Let me see. Thank you is *spasibo*."

"Yes. Very good. *Spasibo*."

"And excuse me is *izvinitye*."

"Almost. Say it this way."

It was my third Russian lesson with Professor Donskoy. I had sought him out at the University of Maine's extension center in Cabot Cove after receiving an invitation to meet in Washington, D.C., and then in Moscow with a dozen representatives of the Russian publishing industry. It was an exchange program of sorts, conceived and arranged by the Commerce Department. That I was chosen to be a part of the American delegation was flattering, to say the least.

Professor Donskoy refilled our teacups in his cluttered office. He looked like a college professor, features hawklike, hair white and flowing, patches on the elbows of his tweed jacket, a rack of pipes on a paper-strewn desk. He'd been recommended to me by one of my good friends Dr. Seth Hazlitt, who was the professor's primary care physician. Seth was right. Donskoy was a wonderful teacher. The problem was his student—me. Learning even rudimentary Russian was proving to be a daunting task.

"Don't be discouraged," Donskoy said at the end of that day's lesson. "You're doing better than you think you are. Now, this is the vocabulary list to work on before we meet again. When is that?"

He also possessed a slight forgetfulness, adding to his professorial image.

"Day after tomorrow," I said.

"Ah, yes. Day after tomorrow. I'd better make a note on my calendar."

I'd been referred to Professor Donskoy in early spring in Cabot Cove, my home for many years. Spring was a welcome change of season after a harsh winter in which we almost broke our all-time snowfall record. I'd passed most of the winter working on my latest murder mystery novel, intending to take off April and May to simply enjoy the blossoming of flowers and the gradual, revitalizing change from frigid temperatures to milder air. But then came the call from my agent in New York, Matt Miller, about having been invited by our government to join in the exchange project with Russian publishers.

"What's the purpose of it?"

"To foster better relations, and to help the Russians develop a viable publishing industry in its new democracy. An added plus might be to get them to stop publishing American works without paying for the rights."

"They still do that?" I asked.

"Afraid so, although not as blatantly. This is a real honor, Jess. You'll be one of only a few authors included in the group. Most are publishing execs, including your publisher."

"Vaughan is going?"

"Certainly is. You'll be in very good company."

Matt outlined the basic schedule for me. The group from both sides of the Atlantic would gather in Washington for three days of talks, woven into a hectic round of receptions, dinners, and meetings with top American officials, including a visit to the White House where the president of the United States, Paul Singleton, would personally greet us.

"A photo op for him," Miller said, laughing.

"I don't care *why* he's seeing us," I said. "I've never been to the White House, never met a president, or a vice-president for that matter. It's exciting."

"You'll do it?"

"Of course I will. We go to Moscow after the Washington meetings?"

"Yes. I'll have the official from Commerce send you the invitation. All you have to do is RSVP, although I admit I told him you'd accept. His name is Roberts. Sam Roberts. Very high up in the Commerce Department."

"I'll look forward to receiving the invitation, Matt. Thanks for the call."

"My pleasure. How's the weather up there?"

"Delightful, although there's still time for more snow. You know Maine and its weather."

"That's why I don't live there," he said. "If my business didn't depend on being in New York, you'd find me on some sunny Caribbean island. Take care, Jess. We'll talk again soon."

Later that morning, I headed for my local bookstore, owned by a friend, Roberta Dougherty.

"Good morning, Jessica," she said brightly. "What brings you in this morning?"

I told her of my agent's call, and of my pending trip to Washington and Moscow.

"Sounds fascinating."

"Except I don't speak a word of Russian."

"Do you have to? They'll have translators."

"You're right, of course, Roberta. But I'd like to at least try to learn a few phrases. You know, good morning, thank you, excuse me, which way to the ladies' room?"

She laughed. "Now you're getting to the important stuff." She went to a shelf in the cozy shop, pulled two books down, and handed them to me. They were written to help Americans navigate the Russian language.

"Just what I'm looking for," I said. "Better pick up a good guidebook, too."

"I have just the thing," she replied, fetching two fat, lavishly illustrated guides.

I paid, left the shop, and stopped in at Charlene Sassi's bakery where I bought a blueberry scone.

"What's new?" Charlene asked.

I told her.

"Wow! I've always wanted to meet a president."

"Me, too," I said.

"Better get used to fattening food, Jess."

"I haven't even thought about food."

"Russians have the most fattening diet in the world," she said. "Seventy percent more calories taken in every day than we do."

"Better lose a few pounds before going."

"I hear the food isn't very tasty," she said, making a face to reinforce the comment.

"People still say that about British food," I countered. "I'll find out for myself and report."

Back home again, my scone accompanied by a steaming mug of tea, I browsed my book purchases. The more I read, the higher my excitement level. I would never have chosen to travel to Russia for a vacation. But many of my trips have come about this way, unexpected opportunities generated because of what I do for a living.

I dozed off later that afternoon, only to be awakened ten minutes into my nap by the ringing phone. It was Seth Hazlitt.

"Hello, Seth," I said, trying to force sleep from my voice.

"Woke you, Jessica?"

I had to laugh. "Yes, you did."

"Sorry about that. I was callin' to make sure you'd be at the Chamber dinner this evenin'."

"The Chamber dinner. Good thing you called. I forgot."

I'd joined the Cabot Cove Chamber of Commerce a few years ago, urged by my friend Richard Koser, a top professional photographer who'd taken the photograph of me that appears on each of my books. There isn't much big business in the town, but lots of small ones, shops and services, people like me and Richard working out of our homes. The monthly meetings rotate among a dozen restaurants, and we usually have a speaker.

"Got the mayor as speaker tonight," he said.

"Jim Shevlin will be there?"

"*Ayuh.* Promises to fill us in on how things are progressing with that landfill proposal. Damn fool idea if you ask me."

I'd heard Seth's opposition to the landfill project enough times to not want to hear it again. "Where's dinner tonight?" I asked.

"Lobster Dory. Cocktails at seven."

"I'll see you there."

The Chamber of Commerce dinners represent a highlight of Cabot Cove's winter social calendar. Like bears, we tend to hibernate during the long, cold winter months, venturing out only when necessary. But the hundred-plus members of the Chamber show up on the first Thursday of each month in a festive mood, anxious to see each other, share what's been going on in their lives, and enjoy the food and drink offered by the restaurants. This night was no exception.

"What's this I hear about you going to meet the president, and the president of Russia?" Tim Purdy asked the moment I walked through the door. Tim managed real estate around the country from his Cabot Cove offices.

"How did you hear that?" I asked.

"Russia?" Barbara DePaoli said. She was the Chamber's secretary.

"Charlene told me," Purdy said.

"I heard it from Roberta," said DePaoli. "I was in looking for a book and—"

"Jessica," said the Chamber's president and Cabot Cove's leading dentist, Anthony Colarusso. "Say something in Russian."

14

Amazing, I thought as I handed my coat to the hat-check woman, how efficient and swift is the Cabot Cove grapevine. Tell one person, especially during the winter doldrums, and within hours half the town knows.

"You'll have to be our speaker when you get back," Colarusso said. "Tell us all about it. Get you a drink?"

Seth Hazlitt arrived after the cocktail party was in full swing. With him was Cabot Cove's sheriff, Morton Metzger. Mort wasn't a member of the Chamber, but he often attended our dinners, explaining that it was important to keep up to date on what the town's business leaders were doing. In actuality, Mort attended the dinners because he enjoyed everyone's company, and he always paid for his own dinner, as we all did.

"A word with you, Jessica?" Seth said.

I excused myself from Beth and Peter Mullin, who own a lovely flower and gift shop, Olde Tyme Floral, and followed Seth and Mort to a quiet corner of the room.

"What's this I hear about you goin' to Russia?" Seth asked.

"What you heard is probably true," I said pleasantly.

"Russia?" Mort said.

"Yes, Russia. First to Washington, then to Moscow."

They both measured me with stern expressions.

"Is there a problem?" I asked. "I'm thrilled to have been invited. Aren't you . . . thrilled . . . for me?"

"Worried is more accurate, Mrs. F.," said Mort.

"Worried about what?" I asked.

"Crime, Mrs. F."

"Crime?"

"Evidently you haven't been keepin' up with the news out of Russia," Seth said, his tone that of a scolding parent.

"Oh, I think I have," I said. "I've been reading about the crime problem there. I understand it's pretty bad."

"Worse than that," Seth said. "Show her, Mort."

Sheriff Metzger pulled a folded piece of paper from his uniform jacket pocket, snapped it open with considerable authority, and began reading:

"Eight thousand criminal gangs . . . fifty million dollars a year extorted from businesses . . . forty percent of the economy controlled by the Russian Mafia . . . five hundred contract killings last year, Mrs. F. . . . mob hits . . . bankers, politicians, tourists gunned down . . . slaughter in the streets!"

"Oh, Mort, I know there's a problem there with crime, but—"

"Don't dismiss what he's tellin' you, Jessica," said Seth. "You're puttin' yourself in danger by going to Moscow."

"Everyone in the next room for dinner," Colarusso announced.

"I'll be traveling with representatives from our government," I said, starting to walk away. "Absolutely no danger to anyone in our group."

Seth and Mort flanked me as we headed for the dining room. "I just think—"

Seth was interrupted by my investment advisor of many years, Sam Davis. "Sure you don't want me to go along to help you convert dollars to rubles?" he asked, laughing.

"I wish I could take all of you with me," I said.

Fortunately, talk at dinner eventually drifted from me and my upcoming trip to other topics. Steamed mussels, a crisp Caesar salad, and crab cakes sated everyone's appetite. Over coffee, some Chamber business was conducted, and then our mayor, Jim Shevlin, briefed us on the status of the proposed landfill project that had divided the community in recent months. Seth Hazlitt asked most of the questions following Shevlin's brief talk, none of them intended to put the mayor at ease.

I'd walked to the restaurant. Jack Decker, publisher

of Cabot Cove's monthly magazine, gave me a lift home.

"Seth's really worried about your trip," he said.

"I know. He's such a dear, but he does worry too much at times. Mort has him all riled up with his statistics about crime in Russia. I'm sure his facts and figures are accurate, but it's not as though I'm going there alone. I'll be with dozens of people."

"You know Seth, Jess. The older he gets, the more convinced he is that bad things lurk around every corner. Sounds like a great trip, and honor, for you. Keep in touch. Maybe you'll do a piece for the magazine about the trip."

"Happy to. Thanks for the ride."

My phone was ringing as I walked through my front door. It was Seth Hazlitt.

"Seth, I—"

"No more lectures from me, Jessica. You're all grown up, capable of makin' your own decisions."

"Thank you."

"Heard you mention you'd like to learn a little Russian before going there. Know Professor Donskoy over at the extension?"

"I know *of* him."

"Been a patient 'a mine for a long time. Speaks three or four languages, teaches 'em, too, including

Russian. Thought you might want to take a lesson or two from him."

"What a wonderful idea, Seth. I'll call him first thing in the morning."

Seth gave me the professor's number, told me again why the landfill project had to be stopped—"Jimmy Shevlin's a real nice fella, smart and all, but he can be so damn *jo-jeezly* about this landfill thing."

"He's not *that* ornery, Seth. We'll talk more about it at the town meeting this weekend. In the meantime, this lady in about to get to bed. Good meeting, wasn't it?"

"Perfectly fine, Jessica. Call Professor Donskoy."

"I will. Thanks for the suggestion."

After changing for bed, I turned on the late news. The lead item was about an American businessman from Texas who'd been gunned down outside his Moscow hotel.

Russian authorities say it has all the markings of a mob hit, something happening with frightening regularity these days as Russia struggles to shift from its previous Communist system of government to democracy.

With any luck, Seth and Mort hadn't seen the TV report. If they had, I knew I'd be in for another round of warnings the next time we were together.

I turned off the TV and climbed into bed. I could see through my window that snow had begun to fall. It hadn't been forecast, but this was, after all, Maine. I hoped it would amount to only a dusting. As much as I love snow, enough is enough.

One of the guidebooks said that springtime weather in Russia could be delightful.

A lovely thought.

An American businessman shot to death in Moscow.

Not so lovely a thought.

I fell asleep saying aloud some of the Russian phrases I'd learned from the phrase books I'd bought from Roberta.

"Spasibo." "Izvinitye."

I didn't know the Russian word for *murder* and didn't want to.

Chapter Two

Flying into Washington, D.C., in clear weather lifts my spirits. The approach often takes you down the Potomac River, affording a good look at the magnificent monuments that testify to the democracy we all cherish: the Jefferson and Lincoln memorials, the Mall, the buildings of the Smithsonian Institution, the soaring Washington Monument (will I ever get around to climbing to the top?), the Capitol Building, the new FDR Memorial, and the White House. That our capital has fallen onto such hard financial times is cause for sadness. It truly is a special city, the symbol of our nation, and should be supported as such.

I flew there from Boston. Most of the others in our publishing contingent had traveled from New York. The landing at National Airport was smooth. The sun had begun to set over Washington, putting into motion a dazzling display of lights across the city.

As I exited the jetway, two men in dark suits held up a sign with my name on it. "Mrs. Fletcher?" one said.

"Yes."

"I'm Ed Rodier, Sam Roberts's assistant at the Commerce Department." He extended his hand. "This is Mike Moga. He works for Sam, too."

"Pleased to meet both of you," I said.

"We have a car waiting," Rodier said.

"Wonderful. I was told I'd be met."

"Pleasant flight?" Moga asked as we headed for the baggage area.

"Smooth as silk. Will I be meeting Mr. Roberts this evening?"

"Afraid not. You'll meet him at a breakfast in the morning at the Capitol Building, hosted by members of the House Subcommittee on International Economic Policy, Export and, Trade Promotion."

"Must be an important committee judging from the length of its name. Anything on the agenda for this evening?"

"Oh, yes, ma'am. "You'll be a guest of honor at a cocktail party at the Russian Embassy. After that, a dinner at the National Gallery of Art. By coincidence they're featuring an exhibition of Russian art. And then—"

"And then—to bed, I hope," I said.

Rodier laughed. "Not on the agenda, Mrs. Fletcher, but we'll see if we can work some sleep into the schedule."

The long black limousine was driven by a tall, elderly uniformed gentleman. We left the airport, moved smoothly down the George Washington Memorial Highway, and crossed the Arlington Memorial Bridge into the area of Washington known as Foggy Bottom, home of the State Department and George Washington University.

"It's such a lovely city," I said, more to myself than to the two gentlemen with me in the back of the luxurious vehicle.

"Yes, it is," Rodier said, sighing. "But with lots of problems."

We said little more to each other until the driver pulled up in front of the Madison Hotel, on Fifteenth Street NW, directly across from the Washington *Post*.

"I've never stayed at the Madison," I said, "but always wanted to."

"I think you'll find it a pleasant experience," Moga said. "Very classy. A big favorite with foreign dignitaries, especially the Russians. They like it because it has a top-security floor."

"I thought the cold war was over," I said.

"It is," said Rodier, adding, "in some areas."

I didn't press him for further explanation.

The driver opened the door, and I stepped out, followed by my hosts. We entered the lobby, where I stopped to admire an impressive collection of antique furniture. Everything about the space said "rich."

Rodier went to the desk and told the young woman behind it who I was, and that I was part of the Commerce Department's publishing trade group. "She goes on the master bill," he said.

"Welcome, Mrs. Fletcher," the desk clerk said. "First time with us?"

"Yes."

"Well, we'll do everything we can to make your stay a pleasant one."

"Is everyone from the group staying here?" I asked Rodier.

"Just about. A few of the Russian publishers preferred to be put up by their embassy." He turned to Moga. "Two of them, right?"

"Right."

"Cars will be here in an hour, Mrs. Fletcher, to take you and the others to the reception."

"Then I'd better get to my room and put myself together."

I was taken to a large, lovely room on a high floor at the front of the hotel, overlooking the street. The young bellhop showed me how the TV, thermostat, and other things worked. He refused a tip, saying all gratuities were being paid by our hosts. The moment he was gone, I opened my luggage and took out the clothing I planned to wear that evening. It wasn't easy packing for this trip. We'd be away from home for two weeks, and the schedule sent to me before departure indicated there would be dozens of dressy affairs.

When I arrived in the lobby an hour later, the others had already gathered, including my American publisher of many years, Vaughan Buckley, whose Buckley House is among the industry's most prestigious. It was always good to see him. Not only did he publish me, we'd become best of friends.

"Good to see you," he said, crossing the lobby and kissing my cheek.

"Good to see you, too. Where's Olga?"

"Be down in a minute." His wife had been a top fashion model in New York before meeting and falling in love with the dashing, handsome publisher.

"This is so exciting," I said.

"And worthwhile, Jess. Working with the Russians to build a viable publishing industry can help the country become a democracy, open it up to new ideas after all those years of censorship."

"That *is* worthwhile," I said. "Have you met the Russian publishers?"

"A few. Did Matt Miller tell you we sold rights to your new book to a Russian house?"

"Yes, he did."

"Your Russian publisher is on the trip. Spend some time with him. I think he wants you to come to Russia next year to promote the Russian edition."

"What's his name?"

"Vladislav Staritova. Calls himself Vlady. A funny guy. Drinks vodka like it was water. No surprise for a Russian. He has his wife with him."

"Great. I'll—"

"Jessica." Olga Buckley emerged from the elevator and gave me a hug and kiss.

"Hi," I said. "I was just talking to Vaughan about this wonderful experience."

"I know," she said. "The minute he told me we'd been invited, I started preparing. I even took a crash course in Russian."

I laughed and said, "I hope you did better than I did with mine."

"Everyone, please, the cars are waiting," a young man from Commerce announced.

Our limousines fell in behind two police vehicles, their lights flashing.

"I've never had a police escort before," I said. "I feel like a dignitary."

"You are," Vaughan said. "We all are, at least for two weeks."

"It's a little off-putting," Olga said. "Are we in jeopardy?"

"Of course not," said Vaughan. "It's just a Washington thing. A government thing."

Fifteen minutes later we were waved through the gates of the Russian Embassy on upper Wisconsin Avenue, an imposing complex surrounded by a high steel fence. Remote TV cameras were everywhere. "It's like an armed camp," I whispered to Olga.

"It's the government," Vaughan repeated.

We stepped out of the limousines at the main entrance to the embassy, a huge monochromatic buff building. Young Russian military personnel lined the steps as the Russian ambassador to the United States and his wife descended them, welcomed us in English and Russian, and escorted us inside, where the strains of a string quartet wafted from a distant room.

While we paused in the large, circular marble foyer, I used the time to take in my colleagues. There were about thirty people, including wives of some of the publishers, and the husband of the only female publishing executive. Everyone seemed in good spirits, although the Russians looked fatigued, the result, I assumed, of their long flight to Washington. I'd probably look the same after our flight to Moscow later in the week. The chatter was a mix of English and Russian. As I looked at their faces, I had a reaction I often experience, that despite the unfortunate tendency to stereotype those who aren't just like us, we're all basically the same—human beings speaking different languages and of different skin colors and religious beliefs, but the same—aspiring to the same goals, feeling the same pain, laughing and crying at the same things.

I didn't have much time to dwell on the thought because we were led from the foyer into a ballroom, where the ambassador and his wife headed a long reception line. To the musical group's rendition of a familiar Russian melody, Mussorgsky's *Night on Bald Mountain*, I preceded Vaughan and Olga Buckley as we progressed down the line. A young man in a tuxedo was handling the introductions. I wondered how politicians do it, shaking hundreds, even thousands of hands each day. Obviously, I was not cut out to run for elective office.

As I would quickly learn, socializing with Russians meant that vodka and caviar were never far away. I declined a drink, opting instead for sparkling bottled water, and plucked a smoked salmon on brown bread from a passing tray. Vaughan Buckley raised his glass of vodka: "To the first night of a memorable experience." Olga and I touched rims with him.

"Mr. Buckley," a corpulent gentleman in a tuxedo said. An equally large woman dressed in a sequined purple dress was on his arm.

"Hello, Vlady," Vaughan said. "This is my wife, Olga. And this is your new author, Jessica Fletcher."

Vladislav Staritova bowed and extended his hand, which I took. Mrs. Staritova smiled pleasantly. "*Dobry viecher*," her husband said. "A sincere pleasure."

"Oh, yes. *Dobry viecher*," I said, remembering from my lessons with Professor Donskoy that it meant good evening. "The pleasure is mine. I'm delighted you'll be making my book available to Russian readers."

"And it warms my heart that it will be my publishing company that makes it possible."

The party at the Russian Embassy lasted a little over an hour, not enough time to meet everyone, but a good start. I spent most of the party with Mr. and Mrs. Staritova. They were pleasant conversationalists, although as "Vlady" continued to down shots of chilled vodka served by a waiter who seemed to have become his personal valet, his speech became a little sloppy, his eyes watery. That was all right. The problem was he also increasingly felt the need to touch me to make his point, a hand on the arm or shoulder, a few attempts to hug me when he was expressing pleasure at having bought the rights to my book. I eventually found a reason to break away, and joined a knot of American publishers in another part of the room.

The limousines next took us to the National Gallery of Art for a dinner in its West Wing, where Old Masters are displayed. The East Wing, designed by famed architect I. M. Pei, houses more modern collections.

Tables had been elaborately set in a large space devoted to an exhibition of art by Russian artists whose names I didn't know—Vrubel, Nakst, Somov, and Kustodiev—but who, I was assured, represented an important era in art created around the turn of the century in what was then the Soviet Union. Two contemporary representatives of Russia's creative community, who'd come to Washington as special guests of the National Gallery and the Library of Congress, joined us at dinner. One, a graphic artist, was a handsome young man with jet black hair and sensuous dark brown eyes that were in constant motion. The other, a writer, was older; I judged him to be in his early sixties. He was a short man with noticeably bowed legs and unruly steel gray hair. His glasses had extremely thick lenses. I was seated next to him at dinner. His English vocabulary was good, his accent heavy. His name was Dimitri Rublev.

Seated on the other side of me was Vladislav Staritova, who insisted I call him Vlady. He continued to down vodka as though it were water, although he didn't seem to have become more inebriated than he'd been at the Russian Embassy.

"I am flattered to be seated next to you," the Russian writer, Rublev, said. "You are a very famous author."

"Thank you," I said.

"I am not so famous," he said.

"What sort of books do you write?" I asked.

"Poetry, mostly. But I have just finished a novel, my first."

"That's wonderful."

"It is a murder mystery."

"Then I'm in trouble."

"Why do you say that?"

"I'll have to compete with you for readers." He seemed to take me seriously. "I was only joking," I said.

We both laughed.

"Mine is a political mystery, Mrs. Fletcher."

"Oh? Politics as they are today in Russia, or when it was the Soviet Union?"

"It takes place in today's Russia. The *new* Russia." There was sarcasm in his tone.

I looked to Staritova, who was engaged in a conversation with his wife. I asked Rublev, "Is Mr. Staritova your publisher?"

His expression was that of having tasted sour milk. He shook his head and finished a half glass of vodka that had been sitting in front of him.

The dinner was excellent, although I made a silent pledge to go easy on meals for the duration of the trip. These next two weeks could easily undo an entire winter of exercise and healthy eating.

After dinner the curator of the Russian exhibition gave us a tour of the artwork on display. As we moved from painting to painting, I couldn't help but be aware that there were a number of people in the large gallery space who kept an eagle-eye on us. Not unusual, of course. All major museums have large security staffs to ensure no one attempts to steal or deface a work of art. But there were plenty of uniformed guards throughout the National Gallery to see to that.

The men I noticed did not wear uniforms. And they formed two distinct groups.

One group was distinctly American, judging from their clothing, haircuts, and general demeanor. Secret Service? I wondered. No. That elite group of men and women wouldn't be assigned to watch over a trade mission, unless the president and his inner circle were involved.

Plainclothes officers working for the National Gallery? Unlikely.

The second group was comprised of angry-looking younger men whose suits and Slavic faces indicated they were probably Russian. My assumption was that they fulfilled some sort of security role for the Russians taking part in the trade mission. In the days ahead that assumption would be verified.

My attention was diverted from them by a particular painting being discussed by the curator. "Mikhail Vrubel was a tortured artist," he said. "Immensely talented but mad, a man obsessed with the sort of demons you see in this work. He died in nineteen-ten in an asylum after having left a copious amount of work."

"Was he really crazy," an American publisher asked, "or was he put in the asylum for political purposes?"

"I suppose we'll never know," the curator replied.

"Why do you Americans always assume the worst about us?" a Russian publisher asked the American. "What do you think, that every person committed to an asylum is a political prisoner?"

"No," the American replied. "But you must admit

you did use confinement as a way to rid the state of political dissidents."

"Vastly exaggerated," said the Russian, his tone hard.

"Let's continue," the curator said, astutely recognizing that the tension level between the two men was on the rise.

I drifted away from the group led by the curator and went to where my table companion, the writer, Dimitri Rublev, was talking with the Russian graphic artist.

"Hope I'm not interrupting something important," I said.

"Not at all, Mrs. Fletcher," Rublev said.

The graphic artist, whose name I never did catch, excused himself and walked away, leaving me alone with Rublev.

"What a beautiful place this is," I said, indicating the vast gallery.

"*Da.* Yes. We have many wonderful museums in Russia, too."

"So I've heard. I'm anxious to visit some of them when I'm in Moscow—if they give us enough free time to do it."

"The Pushkin is my favorite in Moscow. I hope you are also able to visit St. Petersburg. It is where

I was born. The *Ermitazh* is a fine museum, as fine as any in the world."

"The . . . ?"

He smiled and said, "The Hermitage. Excuse me for using Russian."

"No," I said, "excuse me for *not* speaking Russian."

"It is good we have this chance to converse alone, Mrs. Fletcher."

"I'd like to hear more about your novel, Mr. Rublev."

"That is gracious of you, Mrs. Fletcher. Perhaps at another time. I was hoping—" He looked about, as though to ensure that no one was close enough to hear. One of the unidentified men in a suit—American cut—watched us with overt interest from a corner. From another corner one of the Russians, whom I assumed was part of a security detail, also showed interest in what was transpiring.

"You were hoping—?" I said to Rublev.

"I was hoping you would do me a great favor."

"I will if I can," I said.

Another furtive glance about. "I have a close friend in Moscow," he said. "A writer—very talented."

"Oh? What's his name?"

"That is not important for now. Please, I do not wish to be rude but—"

"You don't need to tell me his name if you don't wish to. I just thought—"

"No, no, please do not misunderstand. My friend . . . she will one day be as famous as you."

"Your friend is a woman."

"*Da.* She is a woman. A very beautiful one."

"Beautiful *and* talented. That's a potent combination."

"Would you . . . would you consider taking something to her from me?"

"What do you want me to take?"

"This." He reached into his inside jacket pocket and withdrew a small pink envelope.

"Is it—?" I shook my head and laughed. "I don't mean to pry. Of course I'll take it to her, provided they allow me the time to meet with her."

"Here." He pulled another item from his pocket and handed it to me. It was a slip of paper. Written on it was: *Alexandra Kozhina—14-A Nikolskaya Ulitsa, Kitay Gorod.*

I cocked my head.

"Her name and address. Kitay Gorod is a section of Moscow adjacent to the Kremlin—a very old section of the city. She lives there. I should say that she is an admirer of yours, Mrs. Fletcher. She speaks and reads English. A friend has brought her English copies of all your books. Her ambition is to be as fine a writer as you."

"That's flattering. I will try to get in touch with her and give her the envelope."

"*Spasibo.*"

"*Pazhalsta,*" I responded, pleased that I'd remembered the Russian word for "you're welcome."

Vaughan and Olga joined us, and we chatted about the exhibition of Russian art until an announcement was made that it was time to leave.

"Nightcap?" Vaughan asked as we entered the Madison Hotel.

"I have a feeling we'd better grab sleep whenever we can," I said. "It's an early start tomorrow."

"Just a quick one," Olga said.

"All right."

I raised my glass of club soda with lime in what was only one of dozens of toasts we would make over the next two weeks. "To the end of the first day," I said.

"A worthwhile reason to toast," said Vaughan. "What did you think, Jess?"

"I was impressed. How could I be anything else? Police escorts everywhere. Feted at the Russian Embassy and the National Gallery of Art. And tomorrow, breakfast hosted by a congressional subcommittee, and a meeting with the president of the United States. What's at night?"

"Russian ballet at the Kennedy Center," Olga said.

"Wow! Yes, I am very impressed."

"What did you think of Vlady?" Vaughan asked.

"He's a nice man. Drinks a little."

Vaughan laughed. "Quite an understatement."

"I was interested in the exchange between the American and Russian publisher over that painting by the artist who died in an asylum."

"Started to heat up," Olga said.

"I hope that sort of thing doesn't taint the next two weeks."

"I'm sure it won't," Vaughan said. "We have a lot more in common than we have differences."

"Publishing," I said.

"Yes. Our common bond, no matter what language we speak."

We talked for another half hour before I announced it was past my bedtime. Vaughan paid the check, and we walked to the elevator. The doors slid open, and we stepped past them. As they started to close, I looked across the lobby. Seated in a chair was one of the men who'd been watching us closely at the National Gallery.

"That man," I said.

"Who?" Olga asked.

"He was sitting in the lobby," I said as the elevator started its rise.

"Who was he?" Vaughan asked.

"I don't know. He was at the dinner, kept to himself. There were a few like him."

We stepped out onto our floor.

"I assumed they were part of the security," said Olga.

"They probably were," I said. "Well, let's all get some sleep. See you in the morning."

Chapter Three

I slept soundly and awoke refreshed and ready, indeed anxious to get on with the day. I opened the drapes and looked down to the street, where men and women briskly walked to their day's work. Because the government is Washington's largest employer, it was a safe assumption that most of them were civil servants of one stripe or another.

Ever since I was told I'd be meeting President Singleton, I debated what would be the perfect outfit for such an august occasion: my comfy Maine look—tweed skirt, simple blouse, and cardigan sweater? That would accurately reflect the way I dressed most days back in Cabot Cove. I also considered a business suit—what do they call it? A power outfit? I'd brought one along in case that was the fashion direction in which I decided to lean. Or, of course, there was the possibility of choosing something more dressy.

It was a good thing I was up early because it took an hour of trying on clothing before I settled on what might be called my "Maine uniform." To wear anything else would amount to trying to costume myself; something I assiduously try to avoid. The president of the United States would meet me as he would were he to visit me at home in Maine.

Pleased with my decision—and after multiple checks in the full-length mirror—I headed downstairs to the lobby to meet up with my colleagues for our breakfast at the Capitol. Everyone seemed as rested and energetic as I was. We happily exchanged greetings, in Russian and in English, and climbed into our limousines for the short ride to where the Congress conducts the nation's business. I'm an inveterate watcher of C-SPAN, that wonderful public service TV channel that provides gavel-to-gavel coverage of the House of Representatives and the Senate when those bodies are in session, and so I'm familiar with many of the faces and styles of the men and women elected to those institutions. Meeting some of them in person would be a treat.

Approaching the Capitol generates a sense of awe. Its cast-iron dome rises majestically into the sky over Washington. Atop it is a nineteen-foot bronze statue called "Freedom," also known as "Armed Freedom" because the female figure in flowing robes has in her right hand a sheathed sword, in her left a shield. Her head is crowned with a helmet crested with feathers, which many visitors assume represents the headdress of an Indian warrior. The fact, according to what I'd read, is that the original model for the statue had her wearing a cap representing the freed Roman slaves, the sort of hat worn by extremists in the French Revolution. But when Jefferson Davis, secretary of war in Lincoln's first cabinet, inspected the model, he saw the original cap as representing Yankee subversion, the sort of symbol that incited slaves to rebel. He insisted upon a change, and the pseudo-Indian headdress was substituted. That's one of the things I love about Washington. There is an interesting story to go with every monument, statue, and other symbols of our country's history.

We were led inside the Capitol Building by a tall, distinguished-looking gentleman in an impeccably tailored gray suit. I didn't recognize him as having been part of our group the previous day and evening. Once we were standing in what's called Statuary Hall, in which two statues of famous people from each state are displayed, he said, "My name is Sam Roberts. I head up the Commerce Department's office of intellectual and creative development. Sorry I couldn't be with you last night, but I had other matters to attend to. I'm delighted to have finally caught up with you this morning for what promises to be an interesting, and I hope enjoyable day and evening in Washington. Let me just say before we go to our breakfast that your willingness to devote your time, and expertise in the field of publishing, to this trade mission is, to me, an outstanding example of citizen participation in the important work of government. The distinguished Russian publishing executives with us on this mission are going through a traumatic shift in their nation's form of governing. After years of the Soviet system, they now find themselves functioning in a democracy in which the first election in years has produced a democratically elected government.

"The American publishing industry has enjoyed freedom since the birth of this nation. To share what we have learned over those hundreds of years with our Russian colleagues will not only develop for us a vibrant market for our books, it will certainly help Russian publishers to flourish in their newfound climate of freedom.

"Having said that—and I think I've already taken too much of your valuable time—let me lead you to a breakfast sponsored by the House Subcommittee on International Economic Policy, Export, and Trade Promotion."

We followed Mr. Roberts to the House Restaurant,

a pleasant, sedate room, where tables had been set for our breakfast. As we came through the doorway, we were greeted by a dozen members of the House, including Cabot Cove's congressman, John Baldacci, a Democrat serving his second term. He immediately came up to me, shook my hand, and said, "Always a pleasure to meet a famous citizen from Maine."

"Thank you for those kind words, Congressman," I said, "but one of the nice things about Maine is that fame doesn't follow you around."

"Well put, Mrs. Fletcher."

"Are you a member of the committee hosting the breakfast?" I asked.

"No, but I knew you were part of the trade mission and wanted to personally welcome you to Washington."

A brief moment of cynicism gripped me. *You're here to shake the hand of another potential voter next time you run*, it said to me. I quickly shed that feeling because I'm not comfortable with cynicism. Skepticism is something else.

I took him at his word and said, "It was good of you to take time out of what I'm sure is a very busy schedule."

"We do keep hopping here," he said, smiling. He handed me his card. "My administrative assistant is Larry Benoit. If you need anything while you are in

Washington, call him. Please stop by if you find the time. My office number is on the card."

He wished me a good day and walked away, leaving me to find my name card on one of the tables, each hosted by a member of the House committee sponsoring the breakfast. In my case, I was seated next to a congressman from California who looked as though he was barely old enough to be a member of his high school student government. His name was Joe Galway.

I was relieved that my Russian publisher, Valdislav Staritova, wouldn't be sitting at the same table with me that morning. I didn't dislike him; I'd only spent an hour or so with him, hardly enough to make a judgment. But there was a certain aggressiveness that I found off-putting. I made a silent pledge to myself to be more open and accepting as the trade mission progressed. If only he didn't drink so much.

Breakfast was delicious, and elegantly served. Various representatives of the Commerce Department gave short speeches, all of them focusing upon the need to foster closer working relationships with the Russian publishing industry. I suspected we would hear a lot more of that talk as we continued on our journey, first through Washington, D.C., and then on to Moscow.

Conversation at my table was spirited and competitive, which kept me from doing much observing of others in the room. But at one point when the dialogue shifted to a topic in which I had little interest, I did just that. Vaughan and Olga Buckley were at a table with Sam Roberts and Ed Rodier of the Commerce Department. Also at their table was the chairman of the subcommittee, a southerner with a boombox voice. His back was to me, preventing me from seeing who sat at the table across from him. Vaughan looked in my direction and smiled. I returned the gesture. As I did, the chairman stood and went to another table, leaving me with a clear view of the man who'd been blocked from my view. It was the same person who'd paid such visual attention to me during dinner at the National Gallery, and who'd been sitting in the lobby of the Madison Hotel when we returned there. Who was he? I again wondered. But then the conversation at my table turned to me, and I found myself discussing my writing habits and schedule, which always seems to be of interest to nonwriters. For me, it simply represents a daily routine. But I happily respond to their questions, reliving for them how I spend each working day in Cabot Cove.

After breakfast we were given a brief tour of the ground floor of the Capitol, including the old Senate chamber, where the Supreme Court once met. The building is spectacular, open to visitors from all over the world who wish to step foot into this country's most visible and enduring symbol of its system of government.

"Ready to meet your president?" Vlady Staritova said, coming up behind me and placing his pudgy hand on my shoulder.

"Yes, and very excited, I might say."

"I have never met President Yeltsin," Staritova said. "Ironic, I meet your president, but not my own."

"I wouldn't feel bad about that," I said. "Most Americans never get a chance to meet their president. This is just one of those unusual circumstances."

"Did you vote for him?" Staritova asked.

"We have secret ballots in this country," I said, injecting a little laugh to lighten my rebuff of his question.

"But I am interested in the politics of American authors, especially your politics, Mrs. Fletcher, now that I am about to become one of your publishers."

I said, "I don't think my politics has anything to do with my books. I'm not writing about politics or government. My murder mysteries are distinctly nonpartisan."

He smiled and placed his hand on my shoulder again, then said, "As you wish."

I was saved by the announcement that it was time to take our limousines to the White House. "Mustn't be late," Sam Roberts said. "Among many traits possessed by our sitting president, punctuality is one of them."

"And a good one," Vaughan said. "I can't stand people who are late."

"Vaughan insists getting to airports at least an hour earlier than necessary," Olga said, walking beside me to the door.

"A man after my own heart," I said.

As we stood outside waiting for the limos to pull up, I noticed the man who'd earlier captured my attention. He climbed into a Lincoln Town Car with two other men in suits. I said to Vaughan Buckley, who stood next to me, "See that man getting in the blue car over there?" I pointed.

"Yes?"

"He's the same one I saw in the hotel lobby last night.

Vaughan looked at me quizzically.

"You were seated with him at breakfast."

"That's right. Why so much interest in him, Jess?"

I shrugged. "I just seem to see him everywhere we go."

"Nothing strange about that. He's part of the Commerce Department's mission.

"He is?"

"Yes. Well, he didn't exactly say that."

"What did he say?" I asked. "Did you ask him who he was?"

"No. He introduced himself. His name escapes me. No, he didn't indicate his job, but the fact that he's here must mean he works for Commerce. I'm sure he's not in the publishing business."

We climbed in the limos and headed for 1600 Pennsylvania Avenue. As when approaching the Capitol, seeing the White House caused my heart to trip, and a smile to cross my face. Although I didn't mention it to Mr. Staritova, I had voted for President Paul Singleton, and had done so with enthusiasm. Singleton was a man seemingly untainted by scandal. He'd served with distinction as governor of Pennsylvania for many years before making his run for the White House. I've never claimed to be particularly astute when it came to politics, especially on a national level, but I've always been keenly interested in the politics of Maine, particularly Cabot Cove. But I'd done my homework before deciding for whom to vote as president during the last election, and based upon Paul Singleton's first year in office, I'd made a wise choice.

I was surprised at how quickly we were allowed to pass through the gate to the White House grounds.

Our drivers pulled up in front of the East Entrance where two rigidly erect marines stood on either side of the doors. Two secret service agents came out, followed by an attractive, tall woman wearing a red dress and a red-and-yellow scarf. Once we'd all exited the limos, she introduced herself. "Welcome to the White House," she said brightly. "I'm Pam Prawley, special assistant to the president for cultural affairs. I'll give you a tour of the house before we meet President Singleton. He has a very busy schedule, as you can imagine, but he personally told me this morning how anxious he is to spend time with you. Please follow me—and make yourselves at home. After all, this house belongs to each of you, too." The Russians glanced at each other. "To most of us," Vaughan said in my ear.

The tour lasted almost an hour. Ms. Prawley was extremely knowledgeable, and shared her insight with us. I learned that George Washington was the only president who never lived there; that Andrew Jackson piped in the first running water, Rutherford Hayes introduced the first bathroom and telephone, and Herbert Hoover arranged for the house's first air conditioning; that the house has 132 rooms; and that the coffee urn in the Green Room had been owned by John Adams, the French candlesticks flanking it used by James Madison.

Eventually, we wound up in the Blue Room on what's called the State Floor, often used by Presidents to receive honored guests. It's where the Christmas tree is placed each year, and where portraits of Adams, Jefferson, Monroe, and Tyler proudly hang.

"The President will be here shortly," said Ms. Prawley. She turned to a young man who'd been in the room when we arrived. "This is Mr. Petrov," she said. "He'll translate for any of our Russian guests who wish him to."

A door opened, and we all turned, expecting the president of the United States. Instead, two men and a woman entered. One of the men was the fellow I kept seeing everywhere we went. Why is he in the White House? I mused.

I didn't have much time to ponder the question because the door opened again and President Singleton, accompanied by his wife, strode purposefully into the room. He was taller than I'd anticipated, and thinner. She was even prettier than she appeared on television, and exuded a genuine and gracious warmth.

The president's smile flashed easily as he moved along the informal line we'd formed, shaking hands as he went. The First Lady impressed the Russian members of the group with her ability to converse with them in Russian. I, too, was impressed.

When they reached me, the president said, "This is a real pleasure, Mrs. Fletcher. You're shaking hands with a fan."

Did he mean it? I silently wondered. Other people have told me how much they enjoy my novels, but discussion quickly proves they haven't read any of them. Was the president of the United States about to disappoint me, too?

"I especially enjoyed *Every Day a Little Death*," he said. "That police chief of the small town who was involved in a conspiracy. What was his name?"

"Jenks," I said. "Walter Jenks."

"Yes, Chief Jenks. I once knew a police chief involved in a conspiracy very similar to the one you created."

"Well, Mr. President, I assure you it was purely a creation. The only police chief I've ever known well is the sheriff of my hometown, Cabot Cove, Maine. And the only conspiracy he's ever been involved in— I think—is to make sure he keeps getting invited to our Chamber of Commerce dinners."

Singleton laughed heartily. "Sounds like a positive conspiracy to me," he said.

He had *read my book!*

"Lincoln enjoyed Edgar Allan Poe," he said. "President Clinton preferred the Walter Mosley books. You might say this president leans toward Jessica Fletcher."

"My publisher will be thrilled to know that," I said. I looked back along the line. "That's him there. Vaughan Buckley of Buckley House."

"I'll tell him. And you keep writing those wonderful novels."

Mrs. Singleton, who followed her husband, confirmed to me that he enjoyed ending his long and demanding days by reading murder mysteries, especially those I'd penned.

"I didn't realize you spoke Russian," I said to her.

"Just a little, Mrs. Fletcher. Comes in handy on occasions like this." With that she was on to the next person in line.

But then the president doubled back and said to me, "I must admit I had trouble buying the motivation of the veterinarian for killing his wife in your last book. Why did he?"

"I thought it came out in the final scene. I'd better re-read it."

"I will, too," he said, again moving on.

When President Singleton and the First Lady had personally greeted the last member of the group, an aide appeared at his side and whispered something in his ear.

"Afraid I must bring this to an end," Singleton said. "I know you've heard it many times since arriving here, but what you're doing is of great importance to this country and to Russia's new democracy. My wife and I are avid readers and firmly believe in a free and open press and publishing industry. Enjoy the rest of your stay in Washington and your trip to Moscow. And to the Russian contingent present, may I just say, *spasibo*."

The Russians laughed and responded to the president's use of the Russian word for thank you with a few Russian terms of their own. Amazing, I thought, how taking the time to learn even one word of a foreign language impresses visitors.

Vaughan Buckley came up to me. "The president is a real fan of yours, Jess."

"So he told me."

"If I didn't think it was tacky, I'd try to generate some publicity with it."

"I don't think the president would appreciate it," I said.

"No, I'm sure he wouldn't. Still, nice to know you have fans in high places."

We were led from the Blue Room by Ms. Prawley and out to where our limousines waited. Again, the mysterious gentleman was present. He stood next to the blue Lincoln Town Car that had brought him and the other two men to the White House. As I stared at him, Vaughan asked, "What's wrong?"

His question snapped me out of my trance. "Wrong? Oh, nothing. Nothing at all."

Vaughan looked to where my attention had been concentrated. "That same man."

"Yes."

"Is he bothering you, Jess? I can mention it to Mr. Roberts."

"Oh, no, please don't. He's not bothering me. Hasn't said a word to me. Where are we off to next?"

"Back to the hotel, I think. We have the afternoon to ourselves before dinner and the ballet at Kennedy Center."

"That sounds splendid," I said. "I need a good, long walk on this lovely day, in this lovely city."

"Want company?"

"Actually, I could use some time to myself, Vaughan. Understand?"

"Of course."

Vladislav Staritova and his wife came to where we stood. "It would be our pleasure if you would join us for lunch," Staritova said. "We can discuss plans for publishing you in Russia, Mrs. Fletcher."

Vaughan looked at me with raised eyebrows.

"Thank you," I said, "but I have . . . other plans for lunch."

Vlady bowed slightly. "As you wish. Your president is an impressive man."

"Yes, he is."

"And Mrs. Singleton is so gracious," said Mrs. Staritova.

"A charming hostess," said Vaughan.

"See you at dinner," I said to the Staritovas as I climbed into the back of the limousine with the Buckleys.

"Lunch?" Olga asked.

"Not hungry," I replied.

"Jess is looking for some solitary downtime," Vaughan said.

"A wise decision," Olga said. "I think I'll find a little of that myself. I have the feeling that this might be the last free time we have on the trip."

I went to my room in the Madison, kicked off my shoes, and started reading a new book, *The Rosewood Casket*, by an author I'd recently been enjoying, Sharyn McCrumb. But the sunshine and gentle breeze coming through the partially open window was too compelling.

I put on comfortable walking shoes and set out for the stroll I'd promised myself. It was a beautiful day in Washington. I took deep breaths as I headed south on Fifteenth Street, the Washington Monument in the distance my beacon on the horizon. I reached Mc-

Pherson Square, where I browsed the art in the Franz Bader gallery, the oldest art gallery in the city, then continued walking until Lafayette Park, the scene of many demonstrations because of its location across from the White House, was on my right. It looked inviting. I crossed the street and entered the park. The nice weather had coaxed hundreds of office workers from their offices to enjoy their lunch outdoors. Seeing them eat made me realize I was hungry.

I went to the park's center and paused to admire the statue of Andrew Jackson on horseback as he reviewed the troops before the Battle of New Orleans. I was in the process of deciding which direction would take me to a restaurant in which I could enjoy a simple lunch when someone said my name. I turned and was face-to-face with the man whose constant presence had piqued my interest.

"Hello," I said.

"Lovely day, isn't it?"

"Yes, it is. I'm afraid we haven't met, although you obviously know who I am."

"I certainly do, Mrs. Fletcher. I'm Ward Wenington." He extended his hand, which I took.

"Just taking a walk?" he asked.

"Yes, but seeing all these people enjoying lunch made me hungry."

"I haven't had lunch, either. Mind if I join you?"

"I—who are you, Mr. Wenington?"

He laughed. He was a good-looking, middle-aged man, with a square, rugged face and close-cropped salt-and-pepper hair. His suit was gray and fit his medium build nicely. "You mean who do I work for?"

"That would be a good start."

"The government."

"I gathered that. The Commerce Department?"

"Sometimes."

"Sometimes. The White House?"

"Sometimes."

"Sometimes."

"Sometimes. Lunch? My treat."

"All right."

"The Hay-Adams is right over there." He pointed.

"Nothing that fancy," I said. "I'm not dressed for it."

"Of course you are. The English Grill is pleasant and relatively informal. You can have something simple if you wish."

I almost decided not to go with him. I'd promised myself an afternoon alone. But I was too curious— had been since arriving in Washington—about who he was. And, he obviously wasn't someone to have reservations about being with. After all, he was trustworthy enough to be in the White House in close proximity to the president of the United States.

The oak-paneled lobby of the Hay-Adams was a minimuseum of Medici tapestries, Regency furniture, French Empire candelabras, and stunning Chinese gouaches. Wenington led me downstairs to the English Grill, a handsome room with a Tudor ceiling, wide plank floors, and bookcases holding volumes written about the two men for whom the hotel was named, John Hay, Teddy Roosevelt's secretary of state, and Henry Adams, a great historian. They'd lived side by side; their houses were joined to form the hotel.

The grill was relatively empty, and we took a quiet table in a corner. The menu was typical English pub; I ordered a diet soda and a salad. Wenington opted for a lager and beef pot pie. Once we'd ordered, he sat back, a satisfied smile on his face, and said, "So you're going to Moscow, Mrs. Fletcher."

His comment took me by surprise. Of course I was going to Moscow. He knew that.

I replied, "Are you part of the Commerce Department's team that put this trip together?"

"I played a role," he said, sipping his lager.

"Played a role," I repeated. "Why are you always so evasive when I ask a question about what you do?"

"Excited about the trip?" he asked.

"You followed me to the park."

His grin was charmingly boyish. "Guilty," he said.

"Why?"

"Why did I follow you?"

I laughed, "Yes. Why did you follow me? A fan of my novels?"

"No. I mean, I'm sure I would be, but I don't get to read much fiction."

"Sorry to hear that. What *do* you read?"

"History. Current events."

"Because you're with the government."

"I suppose so."

"What branch of government?" I held up my hand. "I know; sometimes you work for the Commerce Department, sometimes for the White House, sometimes—"

His hand went up. "I deserve the gibes, Mrs. Fletcher. No more gray answers."

"Good."

Our food arrived, and we started in on it.

"You'll be meeting with some pretty important people in Moscow, Mrs. Fletcher."

"I know. I'm looking forward to it."

"Now that the Soviet Union is a thing of the past, people assume the country has become an overnight democracy."

"I don't assume that," I said. "It will take them many years to be able to shift from the old Communist regime to a free society."

"Exactly. I don't know if you're aware that the Communists are still very powerful in Russia. They constitute the majority of the legislature."

"I read that."

"They want their country back, are willing to do anything to achieve that goal."

"Is it possible that Russia could become a Communist country again?" I asked.

Weninton nodded. "Very possible."

"Hmmmmm. This salad is good."

"So's the pot pie. You know, Mrs. Fletcher, being part of a trade delegation like this offers many opportunities."

"I'm aware of that."

"Sometimes there's more to be accomplished than meets the eye."

"Oh?"

"Having a distinguished group such as yours traveling in Russia means you'll be meeting with many government higher-ups there."

"I'm looking forward to that."

"You'll probably end up having private conversations with some of those people."

I waited for him to continue.

"What we ask of our distinguished citizens in that situation is that they remember those conversations, and keep us informed of what transpired."

"Wait a minute," I said, sitting back and holding up a hand. "I have the feeling I'm being recruited to . . . would it be an overstatement to say recruited as a spy?"

His laugh was pleasant, and slightly condescending. "The cold war is over, Mrs. Fletcher. No more real-life spies. John LeCarre keeps them in business, but—"

"Mr. Wenington, I may not be the most politically astute person on earth, but I know the end of the cold war did not put an end to spying."

"Of course it didn't. And no, I'm not asking you to be a spy. I'm only suggesting that when you return from Russia, you make yourself available for a debriefing. You know, what was said during those privileged conversations you had with Russian leaders. By the way, we do this routinely with many Americans traveling abroad."

"I'll certainly consider it," I said. I finished my salad. "Are you asking every American in the group to be debriefed?" I asked.

"Me personally? No. But others will raise the issue with them."

We stood outside the hotel. The sunny skies had turned overcast. We shook hands.

"Thank you for an unexpected and lovely lunch, Mr. Wenington."

"My pleasure. We'll see each other again before you leave for Moscow."

"I have no doubt of that."

I watched him return to Lafayette Park before heading back to the Madison. As I walked there, I was aware that despite having sat with him at lunch, I still didn't know who he worked for.

That was unsettling enough. But what really bothered me was the need I now felt to continually look over my shoulder.

I didn't like that feeling one bit.

Chapter Four

I'd been to the Kennedy Center for the Performing Arts on three other occasions when visiting Washington, which didn't diminish my enthusiasm for this visit. It's a stunning facility, five performing arts facilities housed under its single sprawling roof—the 2,200-seat Opera House; the Concert Hall, home to the famed National Symphony Orchestra; the intimate Terrace Theater, only five hundred seats and a gift to our country from Japan; the Eisenhower Theater in which dramatic offerings are staged, including the Washington Opera; and Theater Lab Et Al, where experimental productions and children's shows are enjoyed.

This night we were treated to an elaborate buffet in a private room on the second floor. Joining us were members of the Russian ballet troupe who would perform later in the evening. A festive atmosphere prevailed in the handsome room. Sam Roberts, our official host from Commerce, flitted from person to person, chatting, asking how we'd spent our free afternoon, and getting feedback from having met President Singleton and the First Lady. There was vodka and Champagne and caviar, of which my soon-to-be Russian publisher, Vlady Staritova, took full advantage.

We settled into prime seats for the performance of Stravinsky's *Jeux de Cartes*, which the program said was written in 1937, and meant *The Card Party* in English. I enjoy the ballet, although I'm not very well versed in it. The dancers were graceful and lovely, the music typically Stravinsky. But it did run long; by the time the troupe came out for its final bow, I was happy to stand and arch my back against a dull ache that had set in.

By now, various members of the publishing contingent had forged friendships. I was invited by two such groups to extend the night with them, but declined. I looked forward to getting into bed and picking up where I'd left off in Sharyn McCrumb's new novel.

Because Vaughan and Olga decided to join others for a little bar-hopping, I found myself alone in a limousine. The driver, a handsome, proper black man, asked me if we were going directly back to the hotel.

"Yes," I said.

But before I got into the vehicle, I looked up into the black, star-studded sky. The clouds had blown away; it was what Seth Hazlitt would term a "fat night."

"I wouldn't mind a half-hour drive," I said, "before going to the Madison. Would you give me a minitour?"

"It would be my pleasure, Mrs. Fletcher. My name is Fred."

We shook hands. "Sure this won't inconvenience you?" I asked.

"My orders are to take you and the others wherever you wish to go, day or night."

"That sounds excessive," I said, "but I won't argue. Where do you suggest we go?"

He frowned and ran his fingertips over his chin. "We could go by the Mall, the Tidal Basin, over to Rosslyn. The view of the capital is nice from that side of the Potomac."

"I'm in your hands," I said. "Mind if I ride up front?"

"Not at all, Mrs. Fletcher. Be easier for me to point things out to you."

Fred drove slowly, identifying various buildings

and monuments as we went. We passed the row of imposing museums along Constitution Avenue—the Museum of American History, the Natural History Museum, and the National Gallery, where we'd enjoyed dinner the night before. He circled the Mall and commented on the famed Air and Space Museum, the Hirshhorn, Museum of African Art, and the Sackler Gallery.

"There's so much culture here," I said.

"It's one of the many nice things about Washington, Mrs. Fletcher. The wife and I, and the grandchildren, always have something to do or see on my days off."

"That's the Tidal Basin over there," he said, pointing, and turning the limo in that direction. "The Jefferson Memorial. My favorite."

He stopped in front of the rotunda dedicated to the third president of the United States, and the author of our Declaration of Independence. It was beautifully lighted, exuding a magnetic pull on me.

"I'd like to see it up close," I said.

"All right," Fred said, getting out and coming around to open the door for me.

"Join me?" I asked.

. "I can't leave the car, Mrs. Fletcher."

"Of course. I'll only be a few minutes."

I stepped up into the rotunda and paused to admire the huge bronze statue of the great man who meant so much to our country. I wasn't the only person to admire him at that moment. A half-dozen tourists were also in the rotunda. One took pictures of others in his party standing in front of the statue of Jefferson.

I drew a deep breath and closed my eyes. It was one of those special moments I would always remember.

I opened my eyes, smiled, and slowly headed back in the direction of the limousine. I'd almost reached it when a woman's voice stopped me in my tracks. It wasn't very loud. It was what she said that impacted me. "Oh, my God!"

I turned in the direction of her voice, which erupted into a scream that cut through the still night, a prolonged, anguished cry. I saw her. She was fifteen feet from me, looking down into the bushes that ring the monument.

I froze for a moment. But then I slowly approached her. I saw that Fred, my driver, had also responded. He was out of the car and running toward me.

I reached the woman. "What is it?" I asked.

She didn't have to answer because I saw what she'd seen. It was a man's body. He was on his side, one arm extended above his head. He wore a suit, shirt, and tie. His feet and legs were partially covered by the underbrush, his face shrouded in shadow.

The woman—she was young—suddenly hugged me. I felt her body shudder. The young man with her, who'd lingered in the rotunda, now joined us. So did Fred. I indicated the body with a downward cast of my eyes. He leaned forward to better see, stood erect again, and said, "I'll call the police from the car. No sense standing here."

"You're right," I said. To the young woman and her male friend, "Come. We'll wait for the police over there."

The police arrived within minutes. After examining the body and securing the scene, a plainclothes detective took statements from me and the young couple.

"You're the famous mystery writer," he said when I gave him my name.

"What I am at this moment," I said, "is a shaken woman. How horrible to have someone killed in such a revered place."

"Why do you say he was 'killed?' " he asked.

"I just assumed it," I replied. "It didn't look to me as though he died of natural causes—heart attack, that sort of thing. He looks as though he'd been dragged into those bushes. Or out of them."

The detective noted what I'd said. The scene had now expanded to include four or five police cars, their flashing red lights creating a macabre kaleido-scope of color and movement, their squawking radios violating the silent sanctity of the Jefferson Memorial.

"How long were you here at the monument?" the detective asked me.

I looked to Fred.

"Ten minutes tops," Fred said. "Less."

"What caused you to see the body, Mrs. Fletcher?"

"This young woman's scream."

"You didn't see anything unusual while you were here? Hear anything? See any suspicious characters who might have done it?"

"No, although I admit I was totally focused on the statue of Mr. Jefferson. Nothing. I heard or saw nothing out of the ordinary. Have you identified him?"

"No, ma'am. Anything else you can add?"

"I'm afraid not."

"By the way, what are you doing in Washington?"

I explained that I was part of the trade mission.

"Going to Moscow, huh?"

"Yes."

"Well, careful there, Mrs. Fletcher. D.C. is Disney-land compared to that city."

Fred drove me away from the Tidal Basin just as the press started to arrive. I sat with him in the car in front of the Madison for a few minutes, neither of us saying anything.

"You'll be all right?" he asked in his deep voice tinged with his southern heritage.

"Yes. Fortunately, or unfortunately, this isn't the first time I've been in the wrong place when a body's been discovered. I suppose we'll read about it in the papers tomorrow."

"I suppose we will."

He escorted me into the hotel, shook my hand, and wished me a good night's sleep—"If that's possible," he added.

"I think it is," I said. "I'm exhausted. Thank you so much, Fred. I'm sorry my little after-hours tour ended up like this for you."

"Good night, Mrs. Fletcher. Try to enjoy the rest of your trip."

I got into bed and attempted to sleep, but the vision of the body at the Jefferson Memorial precluded that. I got up and tried to read, but my concentration just wasn't there.

I finally turned to television, something I seldom do. I flipped through the myriad cable offerings until settling on a twenty-four-hour news channel. I watched it without interest, the events on the screen and the anchor's voice just a blur. Until—

This just in—the body of a man discovered at the Jefferson Memorial only a few hours ago, and reported here, has now been identified.

I became instantly alert and focused.

. . . the man, whose cause of death is still to be determined, has been identified as Ward Wenington, of Rockville, Maryland. Preliminary information is that he was an employee of the State Department, We'll have more on this as details are released.

I turned off the TV, went to the window, looked down at the empty street, then picked up my watch from where I'd placed it on the night table. It was after midnight.

I called the hotel operator. "What room is Mr. and Mrs. Buckley in?" I asked.

I was told.

"Please ring that room for me."

Vaughan picked up immediately.

"Vaughan, it's Jessica. Sorry if I woke you."

"You didn't. We just walked in a few minutes ago. Enjoy your evening?"

"No."

"What's the matter?"

I told him.

"That's terrible," he said. "It's the same man you've been mentioning to me?"

"Yes. I had lunch with him today."

"You did? Why?"

"Buy me a cup of tea downstairs?"

"I'm on my way."

Chapter Five

Vaughan was waiting for me in the bar when I arrived. He ordered a cognac; I asked for tea with lemon.

The bar was virtually empty, and so we had our choice of tables. We chose one in a corner farthest from the door and bar.

"Now, tell me again about this dreadful experience you had tonight," he said in hushed tones.

I leaned across the table and, keeping my voice down, too, recounted what had happened at the Jefferson Memorial. When I was finished, he sat back, rolled his eyes up, and slowly shook his head.

"I know," I said. "Here I go again, tripping over a body. I think I've come across more dead people than characters in my books have. But there's obviously more to it than simply the murder of an ordinary citizen. The news report said Mr. Wenington worked for the State Department. He asked me at lunch to . . . well, in effect to spy for him. Not, for him personally, but for whatever agency he represented."

Vaughan came forward again. "The State Department."

"According to the newscast. But the State Department doesn't have people debriefing American citizens who happen to travel to Russia, does it?"

"I don't know," Vaughan said. "If you mean that all such activities are confined to an agency like the CIA, I think you're wrong. As I understand it, virtually every agency of our government has an intelligence component. It wouldn't surprise me if this Mr. Wenington worked for the State Department in some aspect of intelligence gathering."

"But don't you think it's strange that he followed me into Lafayette Park this afternoon, and now is found murdered at a place where I just happened to end up tonight?"

"Probably coincidence. Look, Olga and I were approached tonight by someone asking us to do the same thing that this Wenington fellow asked you to do. We were told that because the chances were good we would have private conversations with leading Russian officials, we might pick up information that would be useful to this country. They said we'd be debriefed when we came back."

"Was it Wenington who told you that?" I asked.

"No. Someone else, who said he worked for one of the Senate subcommittees having to do with international trade." A small smile crossed Vaughan's face. "I must admit he was smooth. He put it in terms of the need to gather as much information about Russia's industry and commerce in order to help the Russian people develop their democracy. Olga and I accepted what he said. I don't consider myself naive, Jess, but I did buy it. Maybe you should, too. Of course, there is the added complication of this Wenington chap being murdered."

"Just an 'added complication?' I'd say it represents more than that."

"I didn't mean to minimize it."

"I know you didn't. My question is this: Should I go to Mr. Roberts, or some other high official involved with the trade mission, and tell him about my lunch with Wenington and what he asked me to do?"

"I suppose it wouldn't hurt," Vaughan replied. "Chances are the press will report that you were there, which will undoubtedly prompt Roberts, or someone else from Commerce, to bring it up."

I sat back and chewed on my cheek. "I hadn't even

thought of the press reporting that I was there. Do you think that once they do, my participation in this trade mission will be compromised? Maybe I should offer to drop out, go back home to Cabot Cove."

"Absolutely not. All you've done is to be the victim of bad timing. Wrong place, wrong time. I wouldn't give it a second thought as far as the trade mission is concerned. How you handle your personal reaction to such an upsetting event is another question. Would you prefer to go home?"

I'd thought about that ever since the incident at the Jefferson Memorial, and had come to the conclusion that I would not leave the group unless asked to. I told Vaughan this.

"Good. We have one more day here in Washington before leaving for Moscow. As trite as it may sound, I suggest you try to put this thing out of your mind and focus on why we're here, and that we'll soon be climbing on a plane for Moscow."

"How do I handle the press if they try to communicate with me?"

"A-ha. *That* is something I think we should discuss with Sam Roberts. I suspect the Commerce Department, and any other involved agency, would prefer that you not speak with the press about this. But we can get a reading from them in the morning."

The barman served Vaughan's drink and my tea, and we sipped in silence.

"Feeling better?" Vaughan asked.

"Yes. More relaxed. Hot tea always does that for me." I smiled. "Talking to you tends to have the same effect."

He placed one of his hands over mine on the table and said, "Glad I'm a therapeutic force in your life. Shall we meet for an early breakfast?"

"The earlier the better. I didn't check the itinerary. What are we doing on our final day in Washington?"

"A meeting at ten at the Commerce Department. Some sort of a briefing before we head for Moscow."

"The Russians will be there, too?"

"I don't think so. Just the American contingent. *USA Today* is hosting a luncheon for us across the river in their corporate offices. And, let's see . . . the Russians are giving a press conference in the afternoon at the Russian Embassy. I don't think we're required to be there, although maybe we should. A cocktail party at five at the Four Seasons Hotel, hosted by some group that fosters American-Russian relations. Dinner, I don't know about. I'll have to check."

"I'll do that when I get up to the room. Thanks, Vaughan, for spending this time with me."

"Would you expect less from the publisher of the world's greatest mystery writer?"

"You're right. If I were the world's greatest mystery writer, I would expect it. The fact that I'm not— and you do it anyway—makes me feel good. Give Olga a kiss for me." We stood. "Seven? In the restaurant?"

"See you then. And try to get some sleep. A busy day ahead of us."

Chapter Six

When I arrived for breakfast the next morning, I was surprised to see that Olga wasn't with Vaughan. I asked why.

"Running a little late, Jess," he said. "Not unusual for her when there's an early morning getaway. How did you sleep?"

I slid into the chair on the opposite side of the table. "Pretty good, considering what might have kept me awake." I looked across at him. Generally, Vaughan Buckley has a pleasant expression on his face, no matter what the time of day. But this morning I sensed something was wrong. "You seem upset," I said.

He reached down to the floor and picked up a copy of that morning's *Washington Post*. "I hate to be the one to deliver bad news to you, Jess, but better me than someone else." He handed the paper to me.

The lead story on the front page was about the death of Ward Wenington. There was a murky photograph of the crime scene with Mr. Wenington's partially obscured body in the center of it. I looked up at Vaughan. "Why is this upsetting? It's not news to you."

"Read on," he said, as a waiter came to our table. "Your usual?" Vaughan asked.

"Yes, please." I continued to read.

"Orange juice, dry English muffin, and coffee, half regular, half decaf, for both of us," Vaughan said.

I now saw what Vaughan wanted me to see. The article mentioned that the body had been found by mystery writer Jessica Fletcher, who was in Washington as part of a trade mission sponsored by the Commerce Department, and who was scheduled to leave for Moscow later that night.

"Any calls from the press?" Vaughan asked.

I shook my head.

"I'm surprised," he said. "The *Washington Post* is right across the street."

"Let's just count our blessings," I said, dropping the paper to the floor.

Our juice had no sooner been served when a young man entered the dining room, crossed it, and stood above us at the table. We looked up. "Mrs. Fletcher?" he asked.

"Yes."

"I'm Bob Woodstein. *Washington Post.*"

Vaughan and I looked at each other. If this young reporter's arrival weren't so annoying, we might have smiled at the timing of it.

"I'd like a few words with you," Woodstein said. He had an open, pleasant face, with hair a little shaggy around the ears and neck. He had on a well-worn green corduroy jacket, brown-and-white checkered shirt, and skinny maroon tie that was too short for his torso.

"We were just having breakfast," Vaughan said, indignation in his voice. "Perhaps—"

"No, it's quite all right," I said, smiling at the reporter. Please, join us." Vaughan's expression indicated he was not happy with my invitation.

Woodstein sat.

"Would you like some breakfast?" I asked.

"No, thank you. I've already eaten."

"Well," I said, "I suppose you want to talk to me about having been the unfortunate one to stumble across a body last night near the Jefferson Memorial."

"Yes, ma'am," he said, pulling a reporter's notebook from his inside jacket pocket, uncapping a pen, and preparing to write.

"There really isn't much to tell you," I said. "I was being taken on a short tour of Washington at night.

We stopped at the Jefferson Memorial. I got out of the car and went up into the rotunda for a better look. I stayed a few minutes. As I was leaving, I heard a woman say something like, 'Oh, my God,' and then she screamed. She'd been the first one to see the body. My driver came to where we stood. We went back with him to the car and called the police, using nine-one-one, I presume. The police came. I gave a statement. And then I was driven back here to the hotel where I went to bed."

"Were you with the deceased last night?" Woodstein asked.

"No. Why would you think that?"

"Well, it seems that since you had lunch with him yesterday, you might have—"

"How did you know I had lunch with him yesterday?" I asked, unable to keep the surprise from my voice.

"I don't know the source, but someone at the paper told me that. Since you knew him, I thought you might have been together last night."

"Well, I certainly wasn't," I said, now regretting I'd been so quick to invite him to join us.

"Mr. Ward Wenington was with the Defense Intelligence Agency," Woodstein said matter-of-factly, continuing to write.

"I thought he was with the State Department," I said.

"There's some debate about that," the reporter said. He stopped writing and looked up. "I wouldn't mind a cup of coffee."

Vaughan sighed and summoned the waiter.

"You say there's some debate about where Mr. Wenington worked. Why would that be?" I asked. "Wouldn't it be common knowledge? Public record?"

Bob Woodstein hadn't smiled since arriving at our table, but my question elicited a tiny movement of his lips into what might be considered a smirk. "This is Washington, D.C., Mrs. Fletcher. Things aren't as clear-cut as they might be where you come from. Where *do* you come from?"

"Cabot Cove, Maine."

He wrote it down.

"Mr. Woodstein, may I ask you a few questions?"

"Sure."

"How did you know to find me in this restaurant this morning?"

"I knew you were part of the trade delegation to Russia. I checked with Commerce, and they told me just about everybody in the group was staying here at the Madison. I went to the desk and asked them to ring your room. When there was no answer, I figured you might be having breakfast. I know what you look like because I've read a couple of your books, saw your photo on the cover."

"Next question," I said. "Why are you bothering to interview me? What I've told you is exactly what I've told the detectives who were on the scene last night."

"Just hoping, I suppose, that you could tell me something you *didn't* say to them. Murder isn't unusual here in Washington, but it is when you have a world-famous writer—especially a murder mystery writer—be the one discovering the body."

"As I said, I actually didn't discover the body. It was—"

"What was the woman's name who screamed?" Woodstein asked, not looking up from his pad.

"I have no idea," I answered. "You can get that from the police."

"I suppose I should be a little more honest with you Mrs. Fletcher," he said. "The police aren't being very cooperative. Not that that's unique, but in this case there seems to be a real clamp on things. No one will talk about it. Wenington's connection with the Defense Intelligence Agency—"

"Or the State Department," I said.

"Yes, or the State Department, adds a certain mystery to all of this. What's really strange is that nobody seems to know what killed him."

Vaughan, who'd said nothing as he listened to my conversation with Woodstein, now injected himself. "Does that mean he might have died of natural causes?" he asked.

A shrug from the reporter. "I suppose so," he said. "By the way, who are you?"

He'd put the question bluntly, which visibly annoyed Vaughan. Still, my friend and publisher did not vent his pique. He simply answered, "Vaughan Buckley, of Buckley House in New York. I'm Mrs. Fletcher's American publisher."

Woodstein dutifully noted that in his pad, and again turned to me. "What did you and Mr. Wenington talk about at lunch?"

"I'm afraid that is none of your business, Mr. Woodstein." I didn't want to sound too harsh, but at the same time wanted to get across that I was not about to have my privacy invaded by him, or anyone else.

He held up his hand. "No offense, Mrs. Fletcher, but it's my job. You had lunch with someone from the Defense Intelligence Agency—"

"Or the State Department," I said.

"Yes, or the State Department. You had lunch with this person. You're part of a trade mission on your way to Russia. You have lunch with this man from the Defense Intelligence—or State Department—and then you stumble over his body by the Jefferson Memorial that same night. Please don't misunderstand. I'm not trying to make anything of this. But you have to admit, especially because you create plots and stories for your novels, that it does seem sort of . . . well, sort of *mysterious*."

Vaughan said, "Let's get back to what you said about the cause of death not being determined. There was nothing obvious? No bullet hole, or knife sticking out of his back?"

"I don't have the official report," Woodstein said. "As I told you, there's been a lid put on this story. But I have a source over at the ME's office who told me this morning that there is no visible sign of injury to Wenington. I suppose an autopsy will determine cause of death, but that hasn't been done yet."

"I must admit I feel better knowing he hadn't been murdered," I said.

"I didn't tell you that he hadn't been murdered," Woodstein said.

"I realize that, Mr. Woodstein," I said, "but since there was no visible sign of injury, it's fairly safe to assume that he died naturally. He was a relatively young man."

The three of us looked at each other. As we did, I realized that the conclusion I'd reached didn't have a rational foundation.

"About your lunch with Mr. Wenington," Woodstein said.

"I think this session has lasted long enough," Vaughan said. "Mrs. Fletcher's English muffin is now cold. She obviously has nothing else to offer you. I don't wish to be rude, but we have things to talk about. Privately."

Woodstein closed the cover on his notebook and slipped it back into his pocket. "Sure, I understand," he said. "I really appreciate your inviting me to sit down with you this morning. If I have more questions, where can I reach you today?"

I started to answer, but Vaughan interrupted. "Our schedule is determined by the Commerce Department. You can check with them."

"Okay. Will you be at the news conference this afternoon at the Russian Embassy?"

I looked to Vaughan, who answered, "That hasn't been determined. Have a good day, Mr. Woodstein."

We watched the young reporter walk from the room. When he was gone, Vaughan waved to the waiter and asked for fresh English muffins.

"That's all right," I said, picking up a cold half and taking a bite.

"Nonsense," Vaughan said. After telling the waiter what we wanted, he asked, "Mind a suggestion?"

"Of course not."

"If I were you—and, of course, I am not you—if I were you, Jess, I would avoid the press in this city like the plague. Remember, this is Washington, a lovely city and our nation's capital, but also the world's center of intrigue and gossip and grand plots. Obviously, the press wants to make something of your having had lunch with Wenington, turn it into a conspiracy theory. Don't feed it. We only have today and a portion of this evening to get through before leaving for Moscow. Why don't you and I and Olga stick close together for the rest of the day? If other members of the press want to talk to you, I'll run interference, act as your spokesman, your public relations counsel."

"I suppose you're right," I said. "I invited him to join us because it seemed there was absolutely nothing of interest to tell him. But then when he mentioned that he knew I'd had lunch with Wenington . . . It wasn't a planned lunch. I was taking a walk in Lafayette Park. He came up to me, admitted he'd followed me there, and took me for a quick, unplanned luncheon. How would a reporter from the *Washington Post* know that?"

Vaughan signed the check, looked up at me, and said, "Just remember what I said, Jessica. This is Washington. This is where intelligence is a major industry. Buy my suggestion that I take care of any press queries?"

"Absolutely. I won't stray from your side until we get on that plane tonight for Moscow."

"Good."

We stood together in the lobby.

"We have until ten," he said, "before we get picked up to go to the briefing at Commerce. What do you intend to do until then?"

"Hole up in my room, I suppose. I'd take a walk but . . ."

"Just as well you stay incognito. I'll call you when Olga and I are ready to come downstairs. That way we'll arrive together."

He went off to buy a couple of magazines, and I pushed the button for the elevator. When the door opened, I stepped inside. I was the only person in it. I turned and looked back to the lobby. Seated in the same chair where Ward Wenington had sat two nights earlier was a young man in a suit. He didn't look like Wenington, but he was cut from the same mold. Although he held up a newspaper, I had a feeling he wasn't reading it. He was looking over it at me.

The doors slid shut, and I rode up to my floor. I entered my room and noticed that the telephone message light was flashing. I picked up the receiver and punched in the number to access my messages. There were three, two from members of the press. The third was from a man who said his name was Karl Warner. His message was brief. He said he was calling on behalf of the Commerce Department in regard to the briefing that morning, and would I please return his call. He left a number.

I started to dial, but stopped midway and hung up. I didn't know any Karl Warner. If he was from the Commerce Department, I'd undoubtedly meet him at the briefing.

But the truth was that I was reluctant to call him back because the aura of intrigue that seemed to shroud Washington was beginning to get to me. I made a decision on the spot to follow Vaughan's advice and talk to no one without him being present. I didn't like functioning that way. I've always been an open person, quick to give people the benefit of the doubt.

This was different.

As everyone was quick to point out, this was, after all, Washington, D.C.

Chapter Seven

The phone rang a half-dozen times while I waited in my room to rendezvous with Vaughan and Olga. I didn't pick up; I decided to let the voice-mail screen my calls, and to check them just before leaving the room. Above all, I wanted to avoid speaking with the media.

Besides the initial three messages—two from reporters, one from the gentleman who said his name was Karl Warner—the next six were equally split between the press and friends. Vaughan Buckley had called just to see how I was doing and said that since I didn't answer, he assumed I was doing precisely what I was—using the voice-mail system to avoid unwanted conversations.

Seth Hazlitt called from Cabot Cove to wish me bon voyage for my flight to Moscow. And Larry Benoit, administrative assistant to Maine Congressman

Baldacci, called on behalf of the congressman to offer his services if they were needed at any time during the remainder of my stay in Washington.

I didn't return any of them because I had only a few minutes before I was due in the lobby. I'd return Seth's call later in the day, when I found a few free minutes.

"What a horrible experience you've been through," Olga said after we'd settled in the back of the limousine for the short trip to the Commerce Department, on Fourteenth Street, between Constitution Avenue and E Street.

"It *was* upsetting," I said, aware that I made it sound as though it was nothing.

"Is the press on your trail?" Vaughan asked.

"Yes. I had a number of messages from reporters. I didn't return any of them."

"Good for you," Vaughan said.

"What time is our flight tonight?" Olga asked as the limousine pulled up in front of the Department of Commerce.

"Eleven," her husband replied. "From Dulles."

"I'm looking forward to getting on that plane," I said. "Somehow, Washington doesn't have the same appeal it had for me yesterday."

"I wonder why," Vaughan said, laughing and patting my arm.

The Americans in the trade mission had gathered together in a room used by the agency's spokespeople for news conferences. As we stood chatting and waiting for the briefing to begin, Sam Roberts, our official host, came up to where I was talking with Marge Fargo, the only female publishing executive in the group. "Good morning, Mrs. Fletcher," he said. "Can I steal you away for a moment?"

"Of course."

I followed him to a smaller room. The only other person in it was a young woman dressed stylishly in a blue suit with gold buttons, and white blouse. Roberts closed the door and said to her, "Is Karl waiting?"

"Yes, sir, he is."

"Give me five minutes with Mrs. Fletcher, and then ask him to come in."

The moment she was gone, Roberts said, "Sorry about what you had to endure last night, Mrs. Fletcher."

"Just bad timing, I suppose. I hope it doesn't interfere with our plans."

"No reason it should."

"Mr. Wenington was part of this group. I've seen him at just about every event."

"Yes. A very nice guy. Tragic to lose one's life at such a young age."

"I understand the cause of death hasn't been determined."

"I wouldn't know about that," said Roberts. "I'm told you and Ward had lunch yesterday."

I couldn't help but smile. "Word certainly does get around this town, doesn't it?"

"Washington, D.C., has the most efficient grapevine in the world, I'm afraid. I suppose Ward mentioned to you that you'd be debriefed upon returning from Moscow."

"He was more subtle than that," I said. "He asked me if I would *agree* to be debriefed."

"And what was your reaction?"

"I don't think I had one, although I didn't debate it with him. I understand it's a fairly routine thing, to talk to American citizens after they return from a place like Russia to see whether they can provide information that would be useful."

"Exactly. Because of your stature and fame, it's likely you'll be sought out by Russian officials. That's why we think you could be an especially good source of information."

"I must admit I have trouble with the concept," I said. "I thought the purpose of this trade mission was to foster better relations between the publishing industries in both countries, and to help the Russians adjust to their new form of government."

"Oh, but that's exactly the purpose of the mission," said Roberts. "It's just that other . . . how shall I say it? . . . other auxiliary uses can be made of it."

"Like reporting on private conversations? To me, that represents a distasteful breach of confidence."

Roberts's laugh was gentle, and meant to be reassuring. "You don't have to tell us *everything* you discuss with the Russians while you're in Moscow, Mrs. Fletcher. Just what you're comfortable with."

The door opened, and the young woman stepped into the room, followed by a tall, slightly stooped man with heavy black eyebrows and hair that matched in color. Because of his posture, his nondescript gray suit hung awkwardly from him. He wore large, cumbersome molded black shoes that needed a shine.

The young woman left. Sam Roberts said, "Mrs. Fletcher, this is Karl Warner."

The big man extended his hand; my hand was lost in his.

"You left a message at my hotel," I said, somewhat defensive at not having returned it. People who don't return phone calls have always ranked high on my list of annoyances.

"Yes, I did," Warner said. His voice, low and gruff, matched his appearance.

"Sorry I didn't return your call. I was running late and—"

"No need to apologize, Mrs. Fletcher. I just thought I would touch base with you before this morning's briefing."

I hesitated, then asked, "Why did you call me?"

"As I said, just to touch base, to introduce myself before we met in person."

I looked to Sam Roberts, whose furrowed brow and narrowed eyes said he was sizing up the exchange. Realizing I was seeking a comment from him, he said, "Karl worked closely with Ward Wenington."

I quickly asked, "At the State Department? Or is it the Defense Intelligence Agency?"

Roberts and Warner exchanged a quick glance.

"I'll be going with you to Moscow," Warner said, ignoring my question. Evidently, that's the way things are done in Washington, I decided. Tell people only what you wish to tell them, regardless of what you've been asked.

"Are you involved with the Commerce Department's division that deals with publishing and other creative areas?" I asked.

"We work closely with Commerce on such trade missions," Warner answered.

Another evasion.

The question that naturally came to my mind was why I'd been singled out from the rest of the Americans to have this one-on-one chat. As far as I knew, the others were all still in the briefing room. I was about to ask when Warner said, "You'll have to excuse me. I have to be at another meeting."

Another meeting? I didn't realize I'd been summoned to a meeting.

"A pleasure, Mrs. Fletcher," Warner said, again taking my hand in his large, hairy mitt. "I'm sure we'll have an opportunity to have many good conversations over the next week."

"Yes, I'm sure we will."

Warner left. Sam Roberts said to me, "Karl will pick up where Ward Wenington left off, Mrs. Fletcher."

"Meaning what? That he'll be 'debriefing' me after we return?"

"Something like that. In a sense, he'll be assigned to you for the duration of the trip. There are others in similar capacities who'll be staying close to your American colleagues."

"I get the feeling, Mr. Roberts, that people like Ward Wenington, and now this Mr. Warner, play a role quite apart from people on your staff."

"Well, I suppose I'd better get this briefing over

with. Thanks for giving me a few minutes of your time. If you need anything, just holler."

With that, he opened the door and stood aside for me to rejoin the others. No doubt about it. I was becoming increasingly annoyed at the refusal of people to answer simple, direct questions. I suppose it has to do with my Maine heritage. In Cabot Cove questions are answered, usually with honesty and directness. But this wasn't Cabot Cove. This was Washington, D.C., the center of power for the most powerful and influential nation in the world, the United States of America, of which I was a proud citizen.

Better get used to it, I silently reminded myself as we took seats.

Sam Roberts stepped to a podium with a microphone.

Vaughan Buckley leaned over to me and said, "What was that all about?"

"I have no idea," I whispered back. "He said he was sorry for what I experienced last night."

Our hushed conversation ended as Roberts began his briefing, which consisted primarily of comments on Russian etiquette, the sort of meetings and social events we would be attending once we got to Moscow, and a warning about not going off on our own there. He ended with, "I'm sure you're all aware of the death of a government official here in Washington last night. Many of you met Ward Wenington at various functions. As tragic as his death is, it's at least comforting to know that he died of natural causes."

I sat up straight. Roberts had indicated to me in the other room that he knew nothing of how Wenington died.

"You probably know by reading the papers that we have a significant crime problem here in the District of Columbia. But it pales in comparison to the problems the Russians are having with crime in their major cities. My point is that we're asking you to stay together, even when you have free time. We've worked closely with the Russians to make sure that any sightseeing and shopping excursions will be done as a group. Other than that, I again thank you for lending your valuable expertise and time to this very important trade mission. You're providing a significant service to your country."

He started to move away from the podium, stopped, returned, and said, "Oh, one other thing. The cold war may be over, but our two countries are still in a very competitive posture. Unfortunately, the old Soviet spying apparatus is still in place, and used in virtually every circumstance. The point is, your hotel rooms, conference facilities, and even the restaurants you'll enjoy will probably be bugged. Keep that in mind whenever you decide to say something to a colleague you'd just as soon not have the Russians know."

I looked at Vaughan. "He makes it sound as though only the Russians are still spying. But he wants us to—"

I was interrupted by an announcement that we were to leave the room. As we stepped out onto the street, the young *Washington Post* reporter, Bob Woodstein, stood near where our limousines lined up. Two Washington MPD squad cars had now joined the entourage, one at the rear of the limo line, the other at the front. Eight uniformed officers were spread out along the sidewalk. Woodstein tried to approach me, but an officer kept him from doing so. I looked in the other direction to where a mobile television transmission truck was parked, a long telescoping antenna protruding from the roof, a video camera trained on the scene as we exited the building.

Across the street stood Karl Warner. He was with two other men in suits.

Amazing, I thought. The day before it was Ward Wenington. Now it was someone named Karl Warner. Interchangeable suits. But with the same mission?

What was that mission?

That was uppermost in my mind as we climbed into the limos and headed for the bridge that would take us across the river into Rosslyn, Virginia, for lunch with top executives of the newspaper *USA Today*.

I started to comment to Vaughan again about my reaction to what Sam Roberts had said about Russian spying, and that our hotel rooms and restaurants might be bugged. But I stopped myself and looked about the limousine's passenger compartment. Was there a hidden microphone in it? Was a secret video camera recording everything we said and did?

"Upsetting, what Mr. Roberts had to say about being careful what we say when in Russia," Olga said.

"Traditions die hard," Vaughan said.

"Thank God we live here," Olga said. She leaned forward and looked at me. "Know what I mean, Jess?"

I nodded. But I was really thinking that the old adage, "Silence is Golden," should be our rule—no matter where we were.

Chapter Eight

Lunch with executives of *USA Today* was pleasant, although I was asked by a top editor to comment on the death of Ward Wenington because of my having been there. Vaughan answered for me. "Mrs. Fletcher said everything there is to say to the police."

I managed to add, "Naturally, although I didn't know him, I extend my sympathy to his family."

"But it came over the wire just before you arrived that you'd had lunch with him yesterday in the English Grill at the Hay-Adams."

"I meant to say I didn't know him *well*."

"The purpose of the lunch was—?"

"Nice meeting you," Vaughan told the editor, placing his hand on my elbow and moving me to another group of people standing near a portable bar, including my Russian publisher, Vladislav Staritova.

"Ah, my dear Jessica," he said, extending his arms to embrace me. I kept my distance.

"Life imitates art, huh?" he said. "You are supposed to *write* about finding bodies, not trip over them yourself."

"Jess would just as soon not talk about it, Vlady," Vaughan said.

"I understand. Better to forget it, huh? You need some vodka, Jessica. Vodka helps to forget."

"Thank you, no, Vlady," I said.

"I insist."

He handed me a glass filled with vodka and held up his replenished glass in a toast. "To you, Jessica Fletcher, and a hope there are no bodies for you to find in Moscow." He laughed heartily at what he'd said, and downed the contents of his glass. I discreetly placed my glass on the end of the bar and said I needed to find the ladies' room.

"Enjoying lunch, Mrs. Fletcher?" Karl Warner asked as I passed him.

"Very much so."

"Need anything, let me know."

"Thank you. I will."

Following lunch, we were given a one-hour VIP tour of the Air and Space Museum before heading to the famed Four Seasons Hotel on the edge of Georgetown for yet another social gathering, this hosted by the nonprofit group whose mission was to foster American-Russian relations. By the time we were ready to leave, Vlady Staritova, along with other Russians in the delegation, were in a raucous, expansive mood, thanks to the vodka that had been flowing freely all day. I was beginning to worry what the long flight to Moscow would be like.

"They'll probably sleep all the way," Vaughan said when I expressed this to him.

I hoped he was right.

We were on our own for dinner; the limousines would pick us up at the hotel at nine for the trip to Dulles Airport and our Delta Airlines flight to Moscow. Vaughan made reservations for six at the bustling Old Ebbitt Grill, a venerable Washington restaurant that's always been a favorite of his. Service was swift, the simple food excellent.

Appetites sated, and after what seemed an interminable drive, we found ourselves buckling seat belts in a Delta wide-body aircraft and roaring into the black night sky—destination, Moscow.

Within minutes, Washington was but a vague memory. The only thing on my mind was the anticipation of visiting a place I'd never been before. After so many years of reading about the Soviet Union and its secretive, brutal society, to be able to see it in-person was exhilarating. Forgotten was finding Ward

Wenington's body at the Jefferson Memorial, men in suits watching our every move, the round of parties and dinners, and Vladislav Staritova's drunken, often humorous behavior.

I sat next to the only other unaccompanied person on the trip, a lovely older gentleman, Marshall Tracy, who published travel guides. He was a widower, he'd told me, and possessed the sort of charm and manners we seem to have lost in today's society. "Well, we're off," he said after the captain announced we'd reached cruising altitude and that he expected a smooth and uneventful flight.

"Yes, we are," I said. "Have you ever been to Russia?"

"Many times. An intriguing country. It's going through very hard times, trying to adjust to democracy. But I think it will succeed—eventually."

I suddenly remembered I'd never returned Seth Hazlitt's call, and mentioned that to Tracy.

"You can call from the plane," he said.

I sneezed.

"Tissue?" he asked.

"I have some, I said," opening my carry-on bag and extracting my purse, which I rummaged through until coming up with a small pack of Kleenex. As I removed it, another item came with it, falling on my lap. It was the small pink envelope and slip of paper given to me by the Russian writer, Dimitri Rublev, at the National Gallery dinner. I'd forgotten about it. I showed the paper to my seatmate. "Know where this address is in Moscow?" I asked.

He adjusted half-glasses and read it. "Kitay Gorod. Very near the Kremlin."

"I'm supposed to deliver this envelope to someone at this address."

"Ah. A friend?"

"No. It was given me by a Russian writer at the National Gallery dinner. Mr. Rublev."

"I didn't meet him."

I laughed. "I think it's a lady friend of his."

"And you are the courier of romance."

"I didn't think about it in those terms, Mr. Tracy. "What a nice thought."

I replaced the envelope and address in my purse, reclined my seat back, and closed my eyes.

Courier of romance.

Sometimes life can be so good.

Chapter Nine

Moscow

"I can't believe this," I said to the person in front of me.

"Maybe it was better under communism," she said.

We'd arrived at Sheremetyevo II International Airport on time. But now, after standing in line for almost an hour to reach Passport Control, we'd gotten on another line to have our luggage inspected by Russian Customs. When the Russian contingent arrived in Washington, they'd been whisked through the process by officials from the Commerce Department. Evidently, our Russian hosts either hadn't thought that far ahead, or had run into an unbending bureaucracy.

"I am so sorry for this delay," Vlady Staritova said as we stepped through doors to the street where dozens of men shouted *"Taksi! Taksi!"*

"This way," one of a half-dozen men who'd met the plane said, leading us to a fleet of gleaming black Mercedes limousines. Dusk was approaching as the cars roared away from the curb and sped us in the direction of Moscow. My limo was shared by Vaughan and Olga Buckley and Mr. and Mrs. Staritova. I couldn't see myself, but judging from the fatigue on their faces, I could only imagine what I looked like.

We eventually reached our hotel, the Savoy, on a street called Rozhdestvenka. When I learned we'd be staying at the Savoy, I immediately wondered whether it was a sister hotel to London's famed Savoy, one of my favorites. It wasn't. The literature said it had been built in 1912 to commemorate the 300th anniversary of the Romanov dynasty, and was known as the Hotel Berlin for a period of time until the demise of the Soviet Union. It's now a joint venture of a Finnish-Russian consortium, completely renovated and competing for Moscow's growing number of visitors, mostly businesspeople.

We tumbled out of the limousines and followed our hosts inside to a lobby of lavish ceiling paintings, glittering gilded chandeliers, and redwood paneling polished to a burnished glow. As at the airport, checking in took some time. But we were eventually assigned uniformed bellhops who led us to our respective rooms. Before splitting up, we were informed that our best bet for dinner was to order room service, and that breakfast was at seven, to be served in a private conference room.

"Seven?" It was a chorus.

"*Da!*" one of the Russians said. "Seven! There is much to be accomplished."

The hallways were poorly lighted, giving the long walk from the elevator a sense of gloom. But the young man who escorted me was friendly, and spoke excellent English. When he opened the door to my room, light poured out, creating a golden pattern of welcome on the hall carpeting.

"This is mine?" I said, stepping into the foyer of an immense, lavishly furnished and decorated suite. In the center of the expansive living room was a grand piano. I went to it and touched the raised top.

"Purchased especially for Luciano Pavarotti when he performed at the Bolshoi Theater."

"My goodness, I can't imagine why I'd be given this beautiful suite."

"Enjoy it, please. Your luggage will be delivered shortly. My name is Grenedy. Call me if you need anything." He bowed and backed out the door.

I couldn't help but smile at the opulence in which I'd found myself. I had this vision of hotel accommodations in Moscow being depressing and generally

unpleasant. That certainly wasn't the case in this in-
stance. Was everyone in our group assigned to such
a suite? I doubted it; how many suites would feature
a grand piano?

I pulled out the piano bench, sat, and touched a
key. It was a C—it rang out. I'd had piano lessons
as a child, although I hadn't stuck with it. But I believe that musical training makes better writers.
Nothing more disconcerting than a sentence or para-
graph, especially dialogue, whose rhythm isn't right.

I tried to play a simple piece from my childhood—
Chopin—but although I remembered it, my fingers
just wouldn't cooperate. Still, there was something
magical about sitting at the same piano as the great
tenor Pavarotti and pretending to be in Carnegie
Hall, about to finish my concert to a standing
ovation.

That little fantasy eventually wore thin. Where was
my luggage? I'd been in the suite for almost forty-
five minutes. I scrutinized the phone in the living
room, figured out how to ring the front desk, and
did. A woman answered. I asked about my luggage.
She replied in English that there were many guests,
and that my bags would arrive shortly.

Fortunately, I'd carried necessities in a carry-on
bag, as I always do when traveling, and used toiletries to freshen up. I opened the heavy drapes and

looked out over Moscow, now shrouded in darkness. There wasn't much to see. The Savoy is located on a side street; no majestic view of the Kremlin or Moscow River.

I called the desk again twenty minutes later, after my bags still hadn't arrived. "Be patient," I was told.

"I would like to order room service," I said.

My call was transferred.

"Room service," a man said in English, with a heavy accent.

"I would like to order something brought to my room . . . suite. Something light. Appetizers, perhaps."

"Ah, of course. *Zakuski.*"

"Pardon?"

"The appetizers. An assortment?"

"I suppose so."

"*Vodichka,* or the Champagne?"

"Ah, mineral water."

"Of course."

"How long will it be?" I asked.

"Very fast. Soon."

Like my luggage, I thought, hanging up.

I sat at the piano again, but before I could try to pick out another tune, the phone rang.

"Mrs. Fletcher?"

"Yes."

"I am sorry to intrude upon you like this."

"Whom am I speaking with?"

"My name is Alexandra Kozhina," the woman said.

"Yes?"

"I am with a Russian writers' society."

"Oh?"

"Murder mysteries," she said, speaking slowly, forming her words with care.

"And?"

"You were told, yes?—that you would speak to us?"

"No, I don't think I was," I said.

"*Da.* I mean yes. You are the famous American mystery writer."

"Well, I do write murder mysteries."

"The government—it brings you to Russia? *Da?*"

"That's right. I'm on a trade mission."

"And you will . . . speak . . . address us."

"If I'm told to," I said. "I'll check with my host tomorrow. If I'm to meet with your group—which, by the way, I'd be delighted to do—I'm sure they'll make the necessary arrangements."

"Yes. That would be good. Thank you."

"Your name again?"

"Alexandra Kozhina."

"Well, I—"

Alexandra Kozhina, the name of the woman the Russian writer, Dimitri Rublev, wanted me to look up when in Moscow, and to whom I was to deliver his envelope.

"Ms. Kozhina," I said into the phone.

The line was dead.

Someone knocked at my door. I opened it. A young man with a rolling cart stood in the hall.

"Please, come in," I said.

I'd no sooner closed the door behind him when someone else knocked. It was my luggage.

I fumbled in my purse for tips. We weren't allowed to bring any Russian rubles into the country with us, so all I had were American bills. I held up a few. The smiles on their faces said they didn't have any problem accepting American currency.

Before they left, the young man who'd delivered room service identified each item on the cart. "*Zhulienn,*" he said.

"*Ya nye gavaryu parusski,*" I said, indicating I didn't speak the language.

He grinned. "Mushroom," he managed. "Sauce. Cream. Sour."

"Ah, yes," I said.

"*Krabi.*"

I laughed. "Crab."

He, too, laughed, and went on to point to dishes containing sturgeon, sausage, and caviar, along with a small salad he called *travi*, which I looked up later and learned literally meant "grass."

They left, allowing me to sample what was on the cart. It was all tasty, although the sausage was too fatty for my palate. When I poured from a pitcher I assumed contained mineral water, my breath was taken away. It was vodka. I knew the term *vodichka* meant "darling little water" in Russian, which might have confused the kitchen. Maybe the safe approach was to always order a Coke.

Generally, I like to immediately unpack everything and put it away, but a wave of fatigue washed over me after I'd eaten. I pulled out a nightgown, robe, and slippers from one of my bags, changed into them, and climbed into the king-sized bed in the adjoining bedroom. My thoughts went to the phone call I'd received from the young woman writer, Alexandra Kozhina. Obviously, Dimitri Rublev had told her when I'd be arriving, and where I'd be staying. But I had trouble squaring that with the circumstances. He'd told me to look her up, not the other way around. And why would he be privy to our travel schedule?

I might have pondered those questions a little longer had sleep not invaded. The next thing I knew, it was morning, and my bedside phone was ringing.

"Hello?" I said groggily.

" 'Morning, Jess," Vaughan Buckley said. "Thought I'd ring you in case you didn't leave a wake-up call."

I sat up. "I'm glad you did. I forgot to."

"Breakfast at seven."

"Yes, I know. I'd better get moving."

"Sleep well?"

"Like a rock, although at the moment I don't feel like it."

"Is your room okay?"

"Oh, yes." I laughed. "It defines opulence. A suite. Grand piano and all."

"Grand piano? You'll have to give us a tour after breakfast. See you downstairs."

I unpacked the rest of my things in a hurry, showered, dressed in the day's chosen outfit, and left the suite at the stroke of seven. As I opened the door and stepped into the hall, a man who'd been leaning against the wall, startled at my sudden appearance, stiffened and turned his back to me.

"*Dobraya utra*," I said, passing him.

He returned my good morning in Russian.

At breakfast a stocky, gray-faced older man in a double-breasted brown suit welcomed us to Moscow and laid out our schedule. It was a full day, beginning after breakfast when we would meet with the new government's cultural ministers. Then it was on to a tour of the Museum of the History of Moscow, lunch with government officials at Aragvi, a state-run restaurant, a bus tour of the city, two free hours for shopping, dinner at a sixteenth-century monastery, the performance of a contemporary Russian play at the LenKom Theater, and finally a Russian nightclub. It was exhausting just thinking about it.

Immediately following breakfast, I sought out the gentleman who'd briefed us, Pyotr Belopolsky.

"Mr. Belopolsky," I said, "my name is Jessica Fletcher."

"Ah, yes, Mrs. Fletcher," he said in excellent English, taking my hand. "A distinct pleasure to meet you."

"Thank you. I received a call last night from a woman who is a member of a Russian mystery writer's club."

"Oh?"

"She said arrangements had been made for me to address the group."

"I am not aware of such a plan, Mrs. Fletcher."

"You aren't? Is there someone else who might have made such arrangements?"

"I don't think so. I would have known. But I will ask others and report to you."

"Thank you, Mr. Belopolsky. I appreciate it."

"What was her name?" he asked.

"I think it was—I have it here." I pulled out the slip of paper containing her name and address. "Her name is Alexandra Kozhina."

I detected a flash of recognition on his face. But he said, "No, I do not know of such a person."

"Well, if I'm to address her group, you'll let me know."

"Of course."

As I turned to rejoin the others, Karl Warner, who'd taken the deceased Ward Wenington's place, approached me. If his job was the same as Wenington's, he went about it with more discretion. I hadn't seen him since leaving Washington. He was on the flight, but sat far removed from me.

"Good morning, Mrs. Fletcher," he said.

"Good morning, Mr. Warner."

"Ready for a busy day?"

"I suppose so. They've certainly packed a lot into it."

"How was your evening last night?"

"Fine. I was tired. Enjoyed room service and early to bed."

His grin was lopsided. "Sounds sensible."

"Will you be with us today?" I asked.

"Yup. Can't get rid of me that easy."

"I wasn't suggesting I wanted to," I said. "Any further word on Mr. Wenington's death?"

"No. Take a while I suppose before they determine how he died. Enjoy the day, Mrs. Fletcher. Looks pretty decent outside, considering it's Moscow."

He walked away, and I thought of his final comment. He was obviously no stranger to the city. Working for the U.S. government must take him to many foreign locations, including Russia. What had life been like here when it was the Soviet Union and controlled by Communists? I wondered, grateful I never had to experience it first-hand.

Warner had been right. It was a cool, sunny day in Moscow, with a bracing breeze coming down the street as we waited for our cars to arrive. Vlady Staritova came up to me. I'd noticed at breakfast that his wife wasn't with him. I asked about her.

"Now we are home," he said, "she had other duties to which to attend. But she will join us for dinner."

"Good," I said. "Were you born in Moscow, Vlady?"

"No. Kiev."

"As in chicken Kiev?" I asked.

"*Kievskaya kotleta*," he said with a chuckle, translating the famous chicken dish into Russian. "You have never tasted it until you have tasted it in Kiev."

"I'm sure that's true," I said as the cars came around the corner and pulled up to the curb.

"I want you to visit my office while you are here," he said. "After all, I am now your Russian publisher."

"I'd be pleased to do that," I said, "providing they give us a little time off."

"I will see to it that they do," he said. "I will be riding with you all day. I arranged it."

I smiled sweetly. "That's . . . wonderful."

The day went by quickly. Our hosts were gracious, if not frenetic, as they tried to keep to the schedule. I was glad I'd worn sensible shoes. Aside from the two hours on the bus, we walked everywhere, through the vast museum, around the remarkable Kremlin complex, and up and down city streets during our shopping break, led by a stylishly dressed Russian woman who steered us into selected shops.

We had dinner at U Pirosmani, named after the famed Georgian artist, Niko Pirosmani. It was across a pond from a sixteenth-century monastery, and featured Georgian food, distinctly different, we were told, from cuisine in other regions of the vast country that contained eleven time zones; Dublin is closer to Moscow than many Russian cities.

Our ranks had swelled considerably by the time we arrived at the restaurant. Many Russian publishing executives had traveled to Washington without their wives. Now, in their home city, their spouses had joined them.

There were also a number of others who'd become part of our growing entourage, young men of the type I'd first noticed at the National Gallery of Art dinner in Washington. The difference here was that there were more of them. Karl Warner congregated with a half-dozen other Americans. On the other side of the room stood six or seven young Russian men in suits. I'd come to the conclusion that no matter what their stated roles, they represented security—or were members of their respective country's intelligence apparatus. Either way, my reaction was ambivalent. There was comfort in their presence. Simultaneously, there was something off-putting in their eagle-eyed scrutiny of everything and everyone, particularly the Russians whose basic brooding nature gave them a perpetual threatening and ominous appearance.

As had been the case all along, the event of the moment caused one to forget they were there, and to become immersed in conversation and, always, food and drink.

The menu was presented in Russian on a blackboard. Mr. Belopolsky, the Russian counterpart to the American Sam Roberts in Washington, suggested that he order for us.

"*Zakuski* for everyone," he told the waiter, indicating a variety of appetizers. "Be sure to include plenty *khinkali* and *gruzinskaya kapusta.*"

I would learn when the platters arrived that he'd asked for lots of meat dumplings and marinated red cabbage. It all tasted wonderful, although I kept thinking of Charlene Sassi's admonition about the caloric clout of Russian food.

Accompanying the *zakuski*, of course, was an unending supply of "darling little water"—vodka—and Champagne, which only fueled the ebullient mood at dinner after a long, arduous day.

Vladislav Staritova sat next to me. He'd consumed enough vodka to float the proverbial battleship. His speech was slurred, and he'd reverted to directing terms of endearment at me despite his wife's presence to his immediate right.

"Ah, my favorite," he said, looking at the main course being served—roast chicken smothered in a heavy white sauce. Vlady leaned close and said into my ear, loudly, "Do you know how we Russians slaughter chicken?"

"How?" I said, playing the perfect straightwoman.

"Starvation." He laughed, causing him to go into a coughing fit. He eventually got over it, licked his lips, and said of the plates before us, "You will like this very much, Jessica. A sweet meal for a sweet lady." He winked at me; the back of his hand brushed my thigh, and I moved my chair a few inches away.

I barely touched my entree; I was stuffed from all the rich food that had come before. The vodka and Champagne had loosened everyone's tongues, and the noise level had steadily risen.

A trio of Russian musicians suddenly appeared and started playing, which added to the festive spirit permeating the room. One of the Russian publishers insisted that the wife of an American join him on the dance floor in the center of the horseshoe-table setup. The music had an infectious melody and beat, and we began clapping as the man and woman moved awkwardly to the music.

"Jessica?" Staritova said, pushing himself up and grabbing my hand.

"Oh, no." I said. "Absolutely not."

I heard his wife say, "Sit down you old fool."

He did, to my relief.

His wife's harsh comment had deflated him. He sat dejectedly, eyes focused on his empty plate, mouth moving as though rehearsing a retort. I felt bad for him. He really was a decent sort when not under the influence of "darling little water."

A waiter whisked away our plates, followed by another waiter who placed desserts in front of us, pastries smothered in chocolate sauce and whipped cream. The band played louder. Others joined the couple on the dance floor. I started to feel dizzy and slightly nauseated.

I didn't know the name of the song, but it reached a point where the Russians suddenly yelped some phrase in concert with the musicians.

I considered leaving the table and going to a rest room. It had all been too much—the long flight, all the food and drink—although I'd barely sipped some vodka to be polite to my hosts—the music, the noise, the . . .

I turned to Vlady to excuse myself.

He looked at me. His eyes bulged, his mouth hung open. His face was beet red.

"Are you all right?" I asked.

He replied by squaring himself in his chair, taking a deep and prolonged breath, and pitching forward, his head hitting his dessert plate with a thud. Chocolate syrup and whipped cream gushed from the plate, creating a black-and-white nest for his face.

His wife screamed.

No one heard because of the music and singing.

I turned to a dour young Russian man who'd been seated to my left. He was gone.

"Help!" I shouted, standing.

The music stopped. People turned and looked at me.

I pointed to Staritova's lifeless body.

"He's dead," I said.

And so he was.

Chapter Ten

Chaos erupted once it was evident—and confirmed—that Vladislav Staritova, my Russian publisher, was dead. Women screamed, men evoked God, and restaurant employees stood in stunned silence.

Karl Warner came immediately to me, gripped my elbow with not inconsiderable pressure, and led me to a corner of the large dining room. I looked to Vaughan and Olga Buckley, who stood with others in an opposite corner. I started toward them, but Warner stopped me.

"I want to be with my friends," I said.

Warner said nothing.

"But I—"

A man ran into the room and came to us. "Ready," he announced.

"Let's go," Warner said to me.

"Go where?" I asked.

"Out of here. Come on. The car's waiting."

"What about them?" I asked, indicating the Buckleys and others.

"They'll follow shortly."

"No," I said. "I'm staying with them."

Warner fixed me with a stare that would cut steel. "Please, Mrs. Fletcher, don't argue. It's for your safety."

"My safety? I—"

Hand still holding my elbow, he propelled me across the floor, skirting the tables, and to the door.

"Jessica," Vaughan called.

I stopped, turned, and made a gesture of helplessness.

"Come on," Warner said, even more stern this time.

The limos that had brought us to the restaurant stood at-the-ready, lights on, doors open, engines running. The young Russian men from our group lined the walkway, displaying weapons.

Vaughan Buckley emerged from the restaurant as I was about to get into the back of the car. I shook off Warner's grip on me and took steps in Vaughan's direction.

"What's going on?" he asked.

"Mr. Warner insists I leave with him."

Buckley faced Warner. "She stays with me," he said.

"Look," Warner said, "we have to leave here *now*! You can talk about it back at the hotel. Please, Mr. Buckley, don't interfere."

Vaughan looked on helplessly as Warner guided me into the limo, climbed in beside me, and slammed the door. "Move!" he shouted at the driver. The vehicle lurched forward.

"Where are we going?" I asked, my voice mirroring my upset and concern.

"The hotel."

"But why couldn't I go with my friends?"

"Because this doesn't involve them."

"*What* doesn't involve them? A man died. A heart attack, I suppose. It involves all of us because we were there."

"I'll explain later," Warner said.

"No," I said. "You'll explain now!"

He turned from me and peered out the window. End of conversation. We rode in silence all the way to the Savoy.

Still not saying anything, Warner escorted me to my suite.

"I must tell you, Mr. Warner, that I resent being treated this way."

"You resent being kept safe?" he asked, opening

doors to closets and the bathroom and drawing the drapes tightly shut.

"Mr. Warner," I said, trying to sound as reasonable as possible, "I'm not critical of your doing your job, whatever it is. But Mr, Staritova's unfortunate death tonight was obviously the result of natural causes. I fail to see where my safety is in jeopardy."

He ignored what I said.

"Mr. Warner, why was I whisked out of the restaurant while the others stayed?"

"Excuse me," he said, picking up the phone and dialing a number. "Jeff, Karl here. She's in her suite."

He listened to what Jeff said, whoever *he* was, hung up, and faced me. "Mrs. Fletcher, I have to be somewhere else. You are not to leave the suite."

"Why?"

He walked to the door.

"Mr. Warner," I said, loudly.

He turned, his expression quizzical.

"I insist I be told why I'm being treated this way. I am, after all, an American citizen."

"I'll be back. There'll be someone outside your door. Sorry for being so brusque. I'll explain later."

He left.

I was consumed with frustration and confusion. I hadn't been able to get a straight answer from anyone since arriving in Washington. Ward Wenington had avoided answering even my simplest of questions when it involved who he was, what he did, and why he was with our trade mission.

His successor, Karl Warner, was equally evasive.

Why?

Surely, having someone keel over at a dinner was not cause to treat the situation as though an armed attack were under way.

The vision of Vlady Staritova collapsing next to me at the dinner table generated a pervasive wave of sadness, especially when I thought of his wife. Poor thing. One minute her husband was laughing and drinking and urging me to join him on the dance floor. The next moment he was dead. I wish I'd been a little more gracious to him. I suppose we always wish we'd been more of something, or less, when someone we know dies.

I opened my door. Standing in the dim hallway was the same man who'd been there when I left that morning. I shut the door, then opened it again. He looked Russian to me. He certainly wasn't an American. Why would Karl Warner have a Russian standing guard outside my suite?

But then it occurred to me that because the same man had been there in the morning, chances were he wasn't working for Warner.

Who *was* he working for?

The phone rang.

"Jessica? Vaughan."

"Where are you?" I asked.

"In our room. You all right?"

"Yes. Shaken, of course, but—"

"Why were you rushed out of the restaurant? They detained us outside for fifteen minutes."

"I don't know, Vaughan. I've been asking myself the same question."

"Let's meet downstairs. There's a bar, I think."

"I can't."

"Why not?"

"I can't leave my room. Mr. Warner's orders."

"Who the hell is he to be giving you orders like that?"

"I've asked that question. He ignores it every time."

"Then I'm coming up. What room are you in?"

I told him.

"Be there in ten minutes."

Ten minutes later, the phone rang. It was Vaughan.

"Coming?" I asked.

"No. I tried. There are three goons in suits just outside your elevator. No one's allowed down your hallway."

"I can't believe this," I said.

"I'm trying to reach our Russian host, Belopolsky, and the embassy."

"You say you got as far as my floor. Why are they allowing *you* to leave your room, but not me?"

"We'll find that out, along with answers to other questions. Did you notice anything unusual about Vlady Staritova before he died?"

"No. He was his usual ebullient self. A little drunk. One minute he was asking me to dance; the next minute he was dead. Any speculation on what killed him? Looked like a coronary."

"No idea, Jess. Look, I'll keep trying to get hold of someone to straighten out your situation. In the meantime, sit tight."

"I don't have any choice. Thanks, Vaughan. Keep in touch."

I hung up and paced the living room, stopping occasionally to hit a few dissonant notes on the keyboard. I felt like a caged animal. What had begun as a wonderful trip to an exotic place, and for a worthwhile cause, had suddenly, dramatically, deteriorated into a nightmare.

My thoughts went back to Cabot Cove and my friends there. I hadn't returned Seth Hazlitt's call. I needed to talk to someone far removed from Moscow and the Savoy Hotel, a familiar voice from the place

I love so much. I did a fast calculation; it was morning in Maine.

I dialed the hotel operator and said I wished to place a call to the United States. My assumption was that the phone system in Russia would be bad, another preconceived, stereotypical notion proved wrong. I was speaking with Seth within a minute.

"Jessica," he said. "Thought you didn't get my message. Called you in Washington."

"I know, Seth. Sorry, but I didn't find a minute to get back to you before leaving for Moscow. Am I calling at a bad time?"

"No. Mrs. Jenkins just left. Got a touch 'a the flu. Joe Jenks'll be comin' in any time now. His gout's just gettin' worse, but the damned old fool won't follow the diet. You're calling from Moscow?"

"Yes."

"Enjoyin' your trip, Jessica?"

"Yes. No. Something unexpected has happened."

"Oh? What's that?"

I told him about Vlady Staritova's sudden death that night at dinner.

"Your Russian publisher died?"

"Yes. And so did a man I had lunch with."

"What?"

"You didn't read about my finding his body in Washington?"

"Can't say that I did. Tell me more."

I did.

My friend exhaled loudly.

"Seth?"

"Looks like Mort was right," he said.

"About what?"

"About you goin' to Russia not bein' a particularly smart thing to do."

"Oh, I feel safe enough," I said, looking around the suite in which I'd become a virtual prisoner. "Not to worry."

"Easy for you to say, Jessica."

I didn't argue. "Anyway, Seth, I apologize again for taking so long to get back to you. Have to run."

"Run to where?"

"Ah . . . have to meet Vaughan Buckley and his wife."

"My best to Mr. and Mrs. Buckley."

"I'll tell them. See you soon."

I'd no sooner put down the receiver when it rang.

"Mrs. Fletcher?"

I recognized the voice immediately. It belonged to the young woman, Alexandra Kozhina, to whom I was to deliver the envelope from Dimitri Rublev.

"Ms. Kozhina?"

"*Da*. Yes."

"Ms. Kozhina, I asked the host for the trade mission I'm on whether I was scheduled to speak to your mystery writers' group. He said he knew nothing of it."

There was silence on the other end.

"I have something for you, Ms. Kozhina," I said.

"From Dimitri."

"That's right. He told you I'd be bringing it to Moscow?"

"*Da.*"

"Then I suggest we get together so I can give it to you."

"I would like to do that—very much like to do that."

"As far as I know, I'll be here in Moscow for a few more days. Would you like to come to my hotel? I'm at the Savoy."

"I know that."

"Or, maybe I can find the time to come to you. But I'm still puzzled about my appearance before your group. It seems to me that—"

"I must go, Mrs. Fletcher."

"Wait. Just tell me—"

The click reverberated in my ear.

I called Vaughan's room, but no one was there.

There was a knock at my door.

"Who is it?" I asked without opening it. There was no peephole as found in most hotels.

"Karl Warner, Mrs. Fletcher."

It sounded like him. Still . . .

"Mrs. Fletcher, it's Karl Warner," he repeated.

I slid open the deadbolt and opened the door to the extent the chain allowed. Warner stood there with two other men, both of whom looked Russian to me. There was no doubt about one of them. He wore a blue-and-gray uniform with red lapels and hat band. The other person was in a dark suit, white shirt, and red tie.

"Who's with you?" I asked through the narrow opening.

"Mrs. Fletcher, there's nothing to worry about. They work with me."

That answer might have sufficed under ordinary circumstances, but I still didn't know whom he worked for.

"Mrs. Fletcher?"

"All right," I undid the chain and stepped back to allow them to enter.

Led by Warner, they went to the middle of the living room and looked around as though deciding whether to purchase it or not.

"Don't you think an introduction is in order?" I asked.

"Yes, of course. This is Mr. Sergius," Warner said,

indicating the man in civilian clothes. "And this is Captain Kazakov, Moscow *Militsia*."

I nodded at both. I knew the Russians called their police force *militsia*. Why an officer of that force was in my room at that hour was the next question I asked.

Sergius, reed-thin and with dark, almost black eyes sunk deep in his face, looked at me, smiled, and said, "I fear we are not showing our best face to the lovely lady."

"I don't care about best faces, Mr. Sergius, but I do wonder why you're here. I assume it has to do with the unfortunate incident this evening at the restaurant."

"*Da*. Most unfortunate," Sergius said. "May I sit?" He took a place on a couch and looked at me with an expression that suggested I join him, which I did. Karl Warner perched on the edge of a windowsill, while Captain Kazakov stood at attention next to the grand piano.

"Well?" I said to all three of them. "Will one of you please explain why the death of a publisher, obviously by natural causes, has resulted in my being raced away from the scene and secluded in my hotel room?"

Sergius removed a cigarette from a thin silver case,

held it to his mouth, glanced at me, and asked, "May I?"

"If you insist," I said. I'm very much against smoking, although it has never become a *cause celebre* for me as it has for millions of others. Besides, I learned from the first day in Washington with my Russian publishing counterparts that smoking was an integral part of their lives. They all smoked. When in Rome . . . or Moscow . . .

He lit the cigarette, took a satisfied drag, waved his hand at Warner, and said, "Please, Karl, explain things to the lovely lady."

Warner appeared to be unsure whether he wanted to be thrust into that role. But he pushed himself away from the sill, took a stuffed chair across the coffee table from me, and said, "I know this must be puzzling to you, Mrs. Fletcher, and I apologize for that. But that's the way it had to be."

"That's the way *what* had to be?"

"The secrecy. I had to keep you in the dark until things were in place."

I couldn't help but smile as I said, "You're still keeping me in the dark. I'd really appreciate being told in simple terms what it is that's going on. My Maine heritage coming through, I suppose."

"All right," said Warner. "Mr. Staritova's sudden

death this evening wasn't the result of natural causes."

I leaned forward. "It wasn't? How do you know?"

Warner looked at Sergius before continuing. "There's more to this trade mission, Mrs. Fletcher, than you might know."

"I'm listening," I said.

"It didn't start out that way. I mean, I don't want you to think we knew from the beginning that we'd be . . . deviating from its stated purpose."

"Has it?" I asked. "Deviated?"

"There are forces at work in Russia, Mrs. Fletcher, that would like to see the new democracy fail."

"Such as?"

"The Communists, for one. Organized crime, for another."

I sat back and collected my thoughts. When I had, I said, "I asked how you knew that Mr. Staritova didn't die of natural causes. As usual, you didn't answer my question. I would appreciate it if you would."

Warner's eyes met mine. He didn't flinch from my comment. Instead, he gave out what would pass as a smile, hunched his shoulders as though against a pain in his back or neck, grimaced, and said, "There are things I just can't reveal at this stage."

I stood, went to the door, and said, "Then I suggest

you leave immediately. And tell those men out in the hall to leave, too. I would not have volunteered myself for what I thought was a worthwhile mission for my country and profession, to be treated this way."

They' didn't move.

"Mrs. Fletcher," Sergius said, "your feelings are understandable." Before I could add to his understanding of my feelings, he said, "You will meet with Ms. Kozhina? Yes?"

"Meet with—"

"Please, sit down," Captain Kazakov said, his first words since entering the suite. His deep voice carried the authority of his position. His smile was broad and genuine. "*Pazhalsta,*" he said, repeating his "please" in Russian. He indicated with his hand that I should return to where I'd been sitting before. I reluctantly did.

"Ms. Kozhina," Sergius repeated flatly.

"What about her?" I asked. "No, more important, how do you even *know* about her?"

"That isn't important," Warner said. "What *is* important is that you obviously have a connection with her."

"Connection? With her? You're wrong. She called me here in my room and—"

"We know that, Mrs. Fletcher," said Sergius.

No one said anything else for a moment. During that period of silence the admonition given us by Sam Roberts in Washington—that we should be careful about what we say because of the possibility of being overheard by electronic devices—came back to me. Of course. My phone was probably bugged. The whole suite, maybe. Was there a tiny microphone inside the grand piano that picked up every note of my feeble attempts to create music? The clock radio next to my bed? The lamps, heating and air-conditioning systems, even beneath the carpeting?

Warner seemed to know what I was thinking. He broke the quiet by saying, "The point is, Mrs. Fletcher, we'd like you to go through with your meeting with Ms. Kozhina."

"I don't have a meeting scheduled with her."

"We know," said Warner. "Make one."

"I don't know how to reach her," I said.

I said it based upon not having a phone number for her. But I did have her address. Did they know that? Did they know about the note from Dimitri Rublev that I was to deliver to her? Had I mentioned Rublev and the note to Ms. Kozhina during our two telephone conversations? I couldn't remember for the moment.

I made a decision on the spot to not mention the note unless they brought it up. I also told myself that there was nothing to be gained by continuing to confront them. After all, they were asking me to do nothing more than to call a young female Russian writer, who I intended to meet up with anyway. By morning, I'd be back in the secure comfort of my American friends and could discuss the situation with them, benefit from their sage advice.

"She'll undoubtedly call again," Warner said, confirming that they knew of the two previous calls from her.

"Why is it so important that I meet with her?" I asked. "Who is she? Why are you so interested in her?"

"All you have to do, Mrs. Fletcher, is meet with her, see what she has to say, and remember it."

"Remember what she says?"

"Right," said Warner.

I thought of Ward Wenington's asking me to agree to be "debriefed" upon my return from Russia. But he hadn't said I'd be asked to engage selected, specific Russians in conversation. This was different.

"I ask again," I said. "Why is Ms. Kozhina so important to you? As far as I know, she's just a young mystery writer."

Warner stood, and said, "You've been very cooperative, Mrs. Fletcher, very patient. I assure you it's appreciated."

The Russian *militsia* captain, Kazakov, and Mr. Sergius also stood. Kazakov clicked his heels and bowed slightly. Sergius came to me and extended his hand. "Thank you, Mrs. Fletcher, for allowing us to intrude on your privacy and your evening. I look forward to meeting with you again."

I turned to Karl Warner. "What if I don't wish to meet with Ms. Kozhina? I don't have to, you know. I'm here as part of a trade delegation, not as a set of ears for whatever agency you work for."

His little smile was annoying. He said, "You're absolutely right, Mrs. Fletcher. You have no obligation to do anything beyond meeting with Russian publishers. Of course, your Russian publisher isn't alive anymore, not as of tonight. A good friend of mine, Ward Wenington, is also dead. I'd like to see that no one else dies. Thanks again, Mrs. Fletcher. Oh, I'd appreciate it if you'd not mention any of this to the others. Wouldn't accomplish anything. Good night."

Chapter Eleven

I called Vaughan Buckley a few minutes after the others departed my suite. He was upbeat; he'd just gotten off the phone with not only our Russian host, Mr. Belopolsky, but with an official at the American Embassy. In both cases, Vaughan assured me, immediate action would be taken to ensure that I was not harassed or bothered by individuals who weren't directly involved with the trade mission.

"That's a relief," I said.

"I made a date tomorrow morning for us at the embassy."

"Oh? Is that necessary?"

"It wasn't my idea. The official I spoke with there—his name's Tom Mulligan—is in the economic development office. He asked that we stop by to meet him. Actually, he wants to meet you. He's a fan of your books."

"That's good to hear. What time?"

"Eleven. We have that nine o'clock breakfast meeting with the Russian Publishers' Association. Lunch at one with the editors from *Ogonyok*. A good magazine, Jess. There's a copy in your room. You might want to browse it before tomorrow's lunch. Three million circulation, and v-e-r-y literary. We'll have plenty of time between the morning meeting and lunch to swing by the embassy."

"All this going on despite what happened tonight to poor Vlady," I said.

"Life goes on, Jess. A tragedy to be sure, but—"

"I was told that Vlady's death wasn't—" I stopped myself in midsentence, my eyes flitting about the room.

"You were saying?" Vaughan said. "About Vlady's death?"

"Oh, nothing. I'll tell you in the morning."

"All right. Feel better?"

"Much, although I'm exhausted."

"Belopolsky offers his apologies for our missing the theater and the nightclub."

"That never crossed my mind. Think I'll get to bed. It's been a long day, and tomorrow promises more of the same."

"Sleep tight, Jess. Things will get back to normal in the morning."

I had a lot of trouble sleeping that night. Despite Vaughan's reassuring words, the confusion of the evening stayed with me. Before going to bed, I opened my door and peered into the hall. The man who'd been there all day was gone. I was tempted to go to the elevators to see whether the other men Vaughan had mentioned were still on duty, but decided against it. It was over. Vaughan said it was over.

Still, sleep came only in fits and starts. I lay awake a long time after they left, chewing on everything that had been said, analyzing it, trying to identify the meaning of it. Was it that easy? I wondered, for Belopolsky, and a single embassy official, to call off the dogs, as it were.

But even if that was the case, there was still the deeply troubling assertions made by Karl Warner and his two Russian colleagues.

They'd said that there were forces wanting to thwart Russia's move to democracy, namely the Communists and the mafia. That statement had been uttered in connection with their request that I arrange a meeting with Alexandra Kozhina.

Who was this mysterious young lady? She'd developed, for me, from mystery writer into legitimate mystery woman. What could she possibly have to do with such monumental issues as governments and organized crime?

But what really kept me awake was the comment that Vladislav Staritova, my Russian publisher, hadn't died at dinner from natural causes. How could that be? How could they know the cause of death so soon after it had happened?

Finally, if Karl Warner was correct—that Staritova hadn't died of a coronary or other natural causes—did that have any connection with the death of Ward Wenington?

I didn't have any answers at the moment and wasn't sure I wanted any.

My final question as sleep finally embraced me was whether there was a hidden camera somewhere in the suite, videotaping my every move. I shuddered at the contemplation, pulled the covers up tight around my neck, and closed my eyes.

What had Sir Winston Churchill said? "Russia is a riddle wrapped in a mystery inside an enigma."

He'd receive no argument from me.

Chapter Twelve

The breakfast with the Russian Publishers' Association was held in a handsome old building near the Kremlin. We joined fifty or more Russian publishing executives in a sprawling, domed room with bloodred wallpaper and gold leaf everywhere one looked.

The president of the association began with an expression of remorse for the unfortunate and sudden demise of Vladislav Saritova, whom he termed "an astute judge of literary properties, a guiding light for all Russian publishers, and a devoted and nurturing husband and father."

Vaughan Buckley leaned over to me and asked in a whisper, "What did you start to say last night about Vlady's death?"

I thought back to Sam Roberts's briefing, in which he said even restaurants might be bugged.

"It was nothing," I said, holding my index finger to my lips. "I want to hear what he has to say."

The ensuing breakfast, surprisingly light by Russian culinary standards, was but a backdrop for a succession of speeches, some in English, most in Russian, with a translator helping us understand what was being said.

Karl Warner stood alone in a corner of the room, his eyes on everything and everyone at once. His presence was unnerving, no matter what assurances Vaughan had given me that last night's situation had been resolved. I decided that I needed to air to Vaughan what had transpired in my suite last night, and hoped we'd have the opportunity to find a few private moments before going to the embassy.

"Ladies and gentlemen," the association's president said, "it has been a great honor and privilege to be with my American friends and colleagues this morning. As you can see from your daily activity sheet, the next few hours are yours to enjoy on your own before your scheduled luncheon. This afternoon, we will get down to the reason you are here, to discuss how we might forge close working relationships to benefit us all. Thank you for your kind attention, and enjoy what our city has to offer."

Marge Fargo, the female American publisher, who'd taken on the unofficial role of group leader, stepped to the microphone and said, "We'll be exploring a section of the city right outside this building. We have an English-speaking guide. The walking tour will last approximately an hour. Please, everyone stay together."

Vaughan and I approached Ms. Fargo. Vaughan said, "Marge, Jessica and I have an appointment at the American Embassy. We won't be with you on the tour."

"We're supposed to stay together," she replied. "Remember what Mr. Roberts said at the briefing?"

"Sure," Vaughan said, "but there won't be any problem going to the embassy. I've arranged for a car and driver. We'll catch up with you at the *Ogonyok* lunch."

"Okay," Marge said. "Is there a problem? I mean, having to go to the embassy?"

"Oh, no," I said. "No problem. There's an official there who enjoys my books. Just a courtesy call."

Marge grinned. "You have admirers everywhere you go, Jess. See you at lunch."

Our driver was waiting outside when we exited the building. The sky was low and leaden. Rain was imminent. The driver, a young man in a black uniform and cap, opened the rear door of his BMW sedan, closed it after we were in, and asked where we wished to go.

"The American Embassy, on Novinsky Bulvar," Vaughan said, consulting a piece of paper.

"Yes, sir," said the driver, slipping the car into drive and pulling away from the curb.

"Are you from Moscow?" I asked as he navigated heavy traffic.

"Yes, ma'am," he said, glancing at me over his shoulder. "Born and raised here."

"You've seen lots of changes, I assume," Vaughan offered.

"Very big changes," the driver said.

"For the better?" I asked.

He looked back at me again. "To be honest, no. But I am lucky. I have this car and can make a living. Others—so much hard work and no pay. The government fails. No taxes collected. The crime, it is terrible. I give almost half of what I earn each month to the *mafiya*—for protection. To not pay, I find the windshield smashed, the tires slashed. No, things are not good here."

Vaughan and I rode the rest of the way in silence. How sad, I thought, for an enterprising, hard-working young man to be the victim of common thugs, using threats of force to squeeze money from him.

We pulled up in front of an imposing yellow-and-white building that housed the American Embassy.

A tall black, wrought-iron fence secured it from passersby.

"We're early," I said, checking my watch. We had a half hour before our appointment.

"I'm sure there's a comfortable place inside to wait," Vaughan said. "Or we can stay in the car."

"How about a walk?" I suggested.

Vaughan looked through the window. Rain hadn't yet started to fall. "All right."

"I will be here when you want me," the driver said after opening the door for me. "My name is Ivan."

"Thank you, Ivan."

"Where to?" Vaughan asked.

"Wherever we can talk privately. How about that little park over there across the street?"

We waited until there was a sizable break in traffic before attempting to cross. Once we did, we stepped into a small grassy area dotted with trees. Two benches faced each other, fifteen feet apart. One was occupied; we took the other.

"Gotten over last night?" Vaughan asked.

"No."

"Sorry. You look agitated, nervous as the proverbial cat."

I kept looking about, from the buildings across the street to the trees, and to the couple on the other bench.

"Looking for someone?" Vaughan asked.

"Yes."

"Who?"

"Anyone and everyone."

"Jess—"

I turned to him. "Vaughan, my suite is bugged."

He laughed. "We were told it probably would be."

"But it is. It *really* is."

"Then you'll just have to be careful what you say."

"I get the feeling everything in Moscow is bugged," I said.

"Even here? In this park?"

"Even here." I pointed to the highest floor of the embassy building. "There are microphones that can pick us up whispering from way up there."

"So I've heard."

"From even farther," I added.

"Okay, Jess. You're right. But why is it so important to you? Is there something you want to tell me that you don't want anyone else to hear?"

"Yes."

"And?"

"I was told last night by Karl Warner—he's the one who took Ward Wenington's place—he told me that Vlady Staritova didn't die from natural causes."

Vaughan's brow creased, his eyes narrowed. "Say that again."

"Vlady didn't die of a heart attack or stroke. At least not according to Warner."

"How did he die?"

"I don't know."

Vaughan sat back and looked up through the trees into the darkening sky. He asked without moving, "Why did Warner tell *you* this?"

"That's another thing I want to discuss with you. When we had dinner at the National Gallery in Washington, I sat next to a Russian writer, Dimitri Rublev."

"I met him."

"He's a mystery writer."

"So he said."

"He asked me to do a favor for him when I got to Russia. He has a lady friend here in Moscow. I call her that, although I really don't know what their relationship is. At any rate, her name is Alexandra Kozhina. Rublev gave me an envelope to deliver to her."

"What's in the envelope?"

"I don't know. It's sealed."

"An unusual request, wouldn't you say?"

"I didn't think so at the time. In retrospect, maybe it is."

"Have you met this woman?"

"No. She called me. Twice."

"And?"

"They were abbreviated conversations. She said I was supposed to speak to her writers' group. I checked with Mr. Belopolsky. He didn't know of any such plans for me."

"Strange."

"I thought so. Anyway, when Karl Warner visited me last night, he brought two Russian men with him. One is a high-ranking police officer. I don't know what the other man does. Warner wants me to meet with Ms. Kozhina."

"How did he know about her?"

"Obviously, my phone is tapped. Maybe the entire room."

"We were warned about that."

"A warning easily forgotten, at least for an American."

"Why would Warner want you to meet with her, Jess?"

"I don't know. I asked him, but received the usual evasive nonanswer."

"How did you leave it with him?"

"I believe I said I'd think about it. No, I said I was under no obligation to do anything except as required by being part of the trade mission."

"And you're right," Vaughan said.

"When I told Warner that, he reminded me that

Vlady was dead, and so was Ward Wenington. He said he didn't want to see anyone else killed."

"A veiled threat, I'd say."

"That's the way *I* took it."

I looked across to the couple on the facing bench. They seemed uninterested in us and what we were saying. But my paranoia antenna was fully extended. "What's that old saying?" I asked Vaughan. "Just because you're paranoid doesn't mean someone isn't following you?"

He laughed gently. "Maybe we'd better check beneath this bench."

"Maybe we should."

"Time to get inside," he said, checking his watch.

As we poised to cross the wide boulevard, I saw that our driver, Ivan, had left his car and stood talking to a man in a heavy black overcoat and black slouch hat pulled down low over his forehead.

"Let's go," Vaughan said, taking my hand and leading us through a break in the traffic. We reached the sidewalk and approached a young Marine in uniform standing at attention at the gate. Vaughan told him who we were and why we were there. The Marine used a phone in a covered box to call within. A moment later, we were inside the American Embassy. A man at a desk verified who we were, issued us badges, and instructed another young Marine to take us to Mr. Mulligan's office on the fourth floor.

The embassy was a busy place that morning. Our uniformed escort remained ramrod-straight as he guided us to a sizable anteroom. A stylishly dressed woman sat behind a large wooden desk. The floor was partially covered by a huge circular red-white-and-blue rug.

"Mr. Buckley," the receptionist said, standing and extending her hand. "Mrs. Fletcher. Mr. Mulligan is expecting you. Please wait a moment."

She disappeared inside Mulligan's office, then returned a few seconds later with him at her side. He was a tall, handsome man I judged to be in his early sixties. Although his hair was mostly gray, his mustache was black, and was shaped to come down the sides of his mouth. He wore a tight double-breasted navy blazer, gray slacks with a razor crease, white shirt, and red-and-white striped tie.

"Ah, Mrs. Fletcher," he said, breaking into a toothy smile and shaking my hand. "What a pleasure."

"This is my publisher, Mr. Mulligan, Vaughan Buckley of Buckley House."

They shook hands. "I spoke with you last evening, Mr. Buckley," Mulligan said. "Good of you to come by this morning."

"Our pleasure," Vaughan said.

"Please, sit down," Mulligan said, indicating a pair of red leather wing chairs flanking his highly polished mahogany desk, on which there was only a small stand from which a miniature American flag protruded, a leather writing pad, and a framed photo of what I assumed was his family.

"Coffee, tea?" he asked. "Something stronger? Vodka? We are, after all, in Russia."

Vaughan and I declined.

Mulligan sat, formed a tent beneath his chin with his fingers, looked at me, and said, "I believe I've read all of your books, Mrs. Fletcher. In fact, I brought a couple of them to the office this morning. Would I be too forward in asking you to sign them?"

"Not at all."

"Now," said Mulligan, "I assume the problem of last night was resolved to your satisfaction."

"I suppose it was," I said.

It occurred to me that the only thing Vaughan knew about my situation when he called the embassy last night was that I was being detained from leaving my suite. Yes, my unwanted visitors had left, and the equally unwelcome gentlemen in the hall had also departed. But that was a minor issue compared with other matters raised during the evening, the ones I'd just confided to Vaughan in the park across the street.

Dilemma: Do I confide those same things to Mr. Mulligan?

My answer was no. It had finally sunk in that when dealing with government officials of any ilk, discretion was vastly superior to valor.

"Our Russian friends do things a little differently than we're used to," Mulligan said, falling into a teaching voice. "They've come out of a closed society and are trying to loosen up their system. But old ways die hard. I suppose what I'm saying is that we have to be understanding where certain events are involved."

Vaughan and I waited for his next comment.

"The business last night with Mr. Staritova was most upsetting."

"It certainly was," I said.

"It caused me to reflect on the death of Mr. Wenington back in Washington."

I sat up a little straighter. Where was he going with this?

"I understand you were the unfortunate one to be there when Ward's body was discovered, Mrs. Fletcher."

"That's correct."

"Ward was a good man. It's a real loss."

"Did he work for the embassy?" I asked.

"Not directly. But he acted as liaison on some very important trade missions put together by Commerce."

"Did he work directly for the Commerce Department?" I asked.

"He—I understand you've made some friends while here in Moscow, Mrs. Fletcher."

"I certainly hope so, although I really haven't gotten to know many people aside from the Russian publishers who came to Washington. But I'm looking forward to meeting as many Russians as possible."

"That's a good attitude," Mulligan said. "Too many Americans shy away from getting to know the citizens of countries they visit. It must be exciting for fledgling Russian writers to have the opportunity to learn from someone of your stature."

"Actually, I haven't met any Russian writers yet, Mr. Mulligan. But I—"

I stopped short, realizing I was about to mention Alexandra Kozhina.

I needn't have been concerned because Mulligan raised her name. "I understand you'll be addressing a Russian mystery writers' group," he said.

"That's news to me."

His eyebrows arched. "Oh? I was told it had been arranged through one of the group's members, a Ms. . . ."

I shot a furtive glance at Vaughan, whose lips displayed the slightest trace of a smile.

"Ms. Kozhina?" I ventured.

"Yes. I think that's her name. Kozhina. Her first name is . . . ."

"Alexandra," I said.

"You're way ahead of me," Mulligan said. "But you say you aren't aware of your talk to them."

"Mr. Mulligan," I said, drawing a breath, "would you be good enough to tell me why you, an official at the embassy, would know about Alexandra Kozhina and my supposed relationship with her?"

"Part of my job, Mrs. Fletcher, keeping in touch with what Americans are doing here in Russia."

"I understand that," I said. "But Ms. Kozhina has come up through other channels."

"Oh?"

I had the distinct feeling that his surprise was feigned.

Vaughan said, "I think we've taken enough of Mr. Mulligan's time, Jess."

"I'm sure he's willing to spare us a few more minutes," I said.

Mulligan nodded.

"The situation you helped with last night was unpleasant for me," I said. "I was present when a very nice man, and my Russian publisher, died suddenly.

I was sitting next to him when it happened. I was rushed from the restaurant and told to remain in my hotel room. There were guards outside my door. The man who took me from the restaurant, a Mr. Karl Warner, brought two Russian gentlemen to my room. They obviously knew about Ms. Kozhina because—"

I looked to Vaughan to see what he thought of my continuing. He shrugged and gave me a small nod.

"It's obvious, Mr. Mulligan," I said, "that anything I say in my hotel room, and on the phone there, is being listened to by others."

Mulligan adjusted his lanky frame in his chair. "Mrs. Fletcher, no offense, but I think you might be reading too many cold war spy novels."

"I take no offense, Mr. Mulligan. Yes, I do read spy novels and enjoy them. But I *know* what I say is true. We were briefed before we left Washington to be careful about what we say in our rooms, what we say anywhere, for that matter."

"No harm in being prudent," he said with a wave of his hand.

"Well," Vaughan said, "it's been a pleasure meeting you, Mr. Mulligan. Let me again thank you for straightening out last night's problem. I'm sure it was just a matter of some confusion on the part of certain people."

Mulligan stared across the desk at Vaughan, then at me.

Vaughan stood.

"Please sit down, Mr. Buckley," Mulligan said.

Vaughan glanced at me, then took his chair.

"Your luncheon is at one," Mulligan said.

"That's right," I said.

"So we have a few more minutes to spend together."

Vaughan and I said nothing.

"Would you mind if I had someone else join us?" Mulligan asked.

He got up before we could respond, went to the door, opened it, and said to an unseen person, "Come in."

Karl Warner stepped into the office. Mulligan closed the door and resumed his seat behind the desk. Warner took a slender wooden chair from against a wall and brought it closer to us.

"You've met," Mulligan said.

"We certainly have," I said. "Would you please tell me what's going on."

"Yes, Mrs. Fletcher," Mulligan said. "I suppose it's time we do that—considering we have a favor to ask of you."

Chapter Thirteen

"You don't have to do it, you know," Vaughan said as we rode from the embassy to our luncheon.

"I'm aware of that," I said. "But he was persuasive."

"So's someone selling snake oil. I was surprised when you agreed."

I sensed that Ivan, our driver, was dividing his attention between watching the road and listening to our conversation.

"You do realize, Jess, that—?"

I put my index finger to my lips and shook my head. Ivan's eyes bored holes at me in the rearview mirror. He quickly averted my gaze and focused on the car ahead of us.

Our lunch with the editors of *Ogonyok* was at Glazur, a Danish-Russian joint venture in a nineteenth-century mansion on the Garden Ring. Because it was only possible to hire a car for a full day, we had Ivan for the duration, whether we used him or not. He politely opened the door for us and scurried to do the same with the door leading into the elegant restaurant, tastefully decorated in shades of muted brown and glittering gold. We were early, beating the others by fifteen minutes. The editors were there, however, and warmly greeted us. After seeing that we had drinks—vodka for Vaughan, mineral water for me—they left us alone for a few minutes.

"Back to what I was saying in the car, Jess. Frankly, I think Mulligan and Warner, and whoever else is involved, have a hell of a nerve asking you to take on something that . . . well . . . that could put you in jeopardy."

"You, too, Mr. Buckley," I said. "They chose to include you in the discussion."

"As Mulligan said, to make you feel more secure."

"Which I do, knowing you'll be involved. Tell you what. Let's enjoy the rest of the day. I told Mulligan I'd think about it, which I intend to do. We're on our own for dinner. I suppose we'll have to eat with some of the others. But after that, let's find a quiet, secure place to talk it over."

He raised his glass in a toast.

"What are we toasting?" I asked.

"You. I live a relatively dull existence as a book

publisher. But I get my vicarious thrills through one Jessica Fletcher. You always seem to end up in the middle of some exciting, threatening, and decidedly unusual situations. This certainly ranks as one of them."

Our colleagues drifted into the restaurant after returning from their tour. Marge Fargo came up to Vaughan and me and asked, "Everything go okay at the embassy?"

"Everything went fine," I said.

"Autograph some of your books, Jess?"

"As a matter of fact, I did. Very pleasant experience. I understand the food here is excellent. I'm famished."

The food was as wonderful as its advance billing. We started with *russkaya zakuska*, a beef aspic in which ham, chicken, and tongue had been finely chopped; went on to a main course of *svinina à la gousar*, spicy eggplant cooked with carrots, onion, and a healthy dose of garlic; and topped it off with the Russian version of baked Alaska and very strong coffee.

"I am absolutely stuffed," I announced to my tablemates.

"Do Russians eat like this every day?" Marge Fargo asked a Russian publisher.

"Da," he said, grinning. "But soon your Weight

Watchers will open here and we will all get skinny, like your American models."

We laughed.

The afternoon was spent in meetings with Russian publishers. I felt slightly out of my element. Although most of my professional life has been spent writing books for publishers, their inner workings are a mystery to me. Still, being privy to the discussions was of great interest. They spoke of how to bridge the American-Russian gap in publishing philosophy, ways to jointly develop books that would have an appeal to both nations' readership, and tackled the thorny problem of assuring that authors from both countries were treated fairly when it came to accounting procedures and royalty payments. The latter topic was of particular interest to this writer, now that my books were about to be published in Russia.

Provided, of course, that Vlady Staritova's sudden death didn't change things. Since his death, I hadn't given even a moment's thought to his being my publisher. The only thing that mattered was that he'd died—and, of course, that I'd been told it wasn't from natural causes. Whenever I stopped to ponder that upsetting possibility, my thoughts also went to Ward Wenington. What was the connection between the two deaths? *Was* there a connection?

A cocktail party at the hotel capped off the day's

official activities. Since we were free to make our own dinner plans, Vaughan, Olga, and I made a reservation at the hotel's dining room, aptly named the Savoy Restaurant. We would have preferred to limit it to just the three of us, but others signed on, and by the time we were seated at a large round table, there were eleven of us.

I knew most of our dinner companions, but there was one man I hadn't seen or met before. I judged him to be in his early thirties. His brown hair was close-cropped, and he sported a pencil-line mustache beneath an aquiline nose. I noticed an especially large ring on the pinky of his right hand, a diamond surrounded by rubies. He introduced himself as Peter Lomonosov, and took the seat immediately to my right.

"What publishing house are you with?" I asked as waiters filled our water goblets, then stood ready to take drink orders.

"I am not with a publishing house," he replied pleasantly.

"What is your connection to us?" I asked.

An engaging smile preceded his answer. "I am with the Cultural Exchange Office," he said.

"A government agency?" I asked.

"Yes. We are most anxious to foster cultural exchanges with America. Through such exchanges we strengthen many areas of our relationship."

"I agree with you," I said.

"I am particularly interested in your American jazz. It is very popular here, and we plan to establish a school for young musicians, very much like your . . . Berklee School?"

"In Boston," I said.

"Yes. In Boston."

"That sounds exciting, Mr. Lomonosov."

"Yes, but it is always hard to find the money."

"In America, too," I said.

We didn't have to worry about choosing what to order because a specialty of the Savoy had been pre-ordered for us—a re-creation of one of twelve menus served in 1896 for the coronation of Czar Nicholas II. I wasn't sure I could get through another big meal, but was determined to try.

The restaurant's decor defined opulence, something I might have expected to see in one of St. Petersburg's imperial palaces, at least based on descriptions I'd read. The dining room soon filled up; every other table was taken, and the general atmosphere became festive, enhanced by a group of Russian musicians. I got caught up in the spirit of the evening, the unpleasant events since joining the trade mission forgotten amidst the laughter and conversation.

That pleasant sensation lasted through dessert—until I saw Karl Warner enter the restaurant with three other people. One of them was the gentleman who'd visited me in my suite, Mr. Sergius, whose affiliation and first name had never been given me. The other two people in their party were a man and a woman, elegantly dressed and carrying themselves with matching aplomb. They were escorted to a prime table near a window.

Vaughan noticed I'd seen them, came around behind my chair, and whispered in my ear, "Maybe we should leave, Jess, and find that private place for a talk."

"I was thinking the same thing," I said.

I turned to excuse myself from Lomonosov, but he'd just gotten up from the table and was making his way to where Warner and his companions had just settled in. I watched him navigate tables and waiters until reaching his destination. Warner and the other man stood and shook Lomonosov's hand. The woman extended her hand from where she sat; Lomonosov kissed it.

Nothing strange or untoward about them knowing each other. Still . . .

We made our apologies to the others at the table, left the restaurant, crossed the lobby, and stepped out into the Moscow night. Traffic, vehicular and pedestrian, was heavy. The Savoy was just off Theater Square, and a short walk to the Kremlin, luring tourists headed for plays and concerts, or sightseers out for a glimpse of the impressively lighted Kremlin at night.

"Are we taking a walk?" Olga asked. I wondered whether Vaughan had told her about the conversation at the embassy that morning. If he had, she didn't indicate it.

"I'd love a walk," I said. "The meal was delicious—and obscenely fattening."

Olga laughed, hooked her arm in mine, and with Vaughan on my other flank, we set out for some much needed post-prandial exercise. We'd gone only a block when Olga said, "Vaughan told me about what happened at the embassy this morning."

"I was hoping he would," I said. "What do you think?"

"Mixed emotions, I guess. On the one hand, it sounds downright exciting. How many people get to play spy these days? On the other hand—"

Vaughan interrupted. "It's also fraught with danger."

"Is it?" Olga asked across me.

"I don't know specifically," he said, "but we are, after all, dealing here with unsavory people."

"I'm glad you said 'we're,' " I said. "I never would have even considered it without you."

Olga stopped us. "You didn't say *we* would be involved, Vaughan."

"We wouldn't," he said. "Not you, at least. But Mulligan at the embassy is pretty shrewd. He knew Jess would never agree to it unilaterally. That's why he included me in the conversation."

We resumed our walk.

"I don't like it," Olga said.

"I have such conflicting thoughts," I said. "The way Mr. Mulligan put it, I'd be doing something very valuable for my country. But I've developed this instinctive mistrust of almost every government official I've met since beginning this trade mission."

"Don't become too jaded, Jess," Vaughan said. "You've just had the misfortune of meeting a certain type of government official."

"The president was charming," Olga offered.

"And the First Lady," I said.

A young man wearing a bandana around his head stopped us. "Rubles for cash American," he said. "I give you best deal in Moscow."

We kept walking. Among many things Sam Roberts briefed us about in Washington was to avoid sidewalk money changers. Deal with them and you'd likely end up seeing the inside of a Russian jail.

"Do you know where we are?" Olga asked.

We stopped to take in our surroundings.

"I think we went the wrong way," Vaughan said. "The theater district is in the other direction."

While talking, we'd wandered onto a dimly lighted street with few people.

"Not the best part of town," Olga said. "Let's go."

We turned to retrace our steps in the direction of the hotel.

"Wait!"

We froze at Vaughan's command.

"What?" Olga whispered.

"There," Vaughan said.

We looked in the direction he pointed. A heavyset man in overcoat and fedora, and smoking a cigar, stood beneath a street lamp that cast minimal light down on him. With him was a casually dressed shorter man.

But they weren't the focus of Vaughan's attention. A long black sedan had pulled up to the curb a few feet from the duo on the corner. Both back doors of the vehicle opened, and two men exited from each side. As dim as the light from the street lamp was, it cast enough illumination to kick a reflection off the gleaming metal barrels of the weapons they carried.

The big man saw them coming and dropped his cigar. The smaller man reached into his jacket pocket and withdrew a revolver.

"Good God!" Olga muttered.

"Over here," Vaughan said, pushing us into a doorway strewn with empty bottles and other trash.

We'd no sooner wedged into the cramped space when another automobile roared up, windows down, men hanging out holding automatic weapons. The firing erupted like a tornado, guns going off, men yelling, bullets ricocheting off the concrete above our heads.

It was over as quickly as it had started. We'd crouched as low as possible to avoid being hit. Now we slowly straightened up and peeked around the corner of the doorway. Both vehicles were gone. The two men who'd stood beneath the street lamp lay on the pavement.

"They're dead," Olga gasped.

"Looks that way," Vaughan said. "You all right, Jess?"

"I think so."

We were frozen in shock and fear. One instinct was to go to the fallen men to see if there was anything we could do to help. The opposing pull was to run as fast as possible from the scene.

"Where are the police?" Vaughan muttered.

As he said it, a car with red lights flashing and two-tone siren blaring screeched around the corner and came to a halt.

"Let's get out of here," Olga said, tugging my arm.

"Don't we have an obligation to—?"

"Olga's right," Vaughan said. "It's some sort of mob rub-out. Not our concern."

"You!" an officer said, approaching us.

"Yes?" Vaughan said.

"Americans?"

"Yes," I said.

"You were here?"

"Here?" Olga said. "Where?"

"Here." He pointed to the corner, where other officers leaned over the bodies.

"No," Olga said. "We were . . . we just got here . . . we . . ."

"If you're asking if we were here when it happened, we were," Vaughan said.

"Are they both dead?" I asked.

"*Da.* Come with me."

"We have nothing to offer," Vaughan said. "We might have been here, but we ducked into that doorway and didn't see the actual shooting."

Vaughan's protest fell on deaf bureaucratic Russian ears. The officer, a tall, stern man wearing the same uniform as Captain Kazakov, said, "You will come with me. Now!"

"Hold on."

We turned to see a man approaching, walking at a fast clip.

"I know him," I said. "He—"

The man came up to the police officer and said something to him.

"Who is he?" Olga whispered in my ear.

"He sat next to me at dinner."

"Yes," Vaughan said. "That's right."

"Name is Lomonosov. Something like that."

"Why would *he* just happen to show up?" Vaughan asked.

Lomonosov came to where we stood. "Good evening," he said.

"Hello," I said.

"I did not expect to see you again so soon," he said. "Peter Lomonosov."

"Yes, I know," I said.

"I am afraid you will have to go with him for questioning," he said, pointing to the uniformed officer. "But I will go with you. Just a formality, I assure you."

The officer waved for us to join him on the corner.

"I really don't want to look at the bodies," Olga said.

"I agree," I said.

"Please," Lomonosov said, stepping back and gesturing with his hand that we should follow the officer.

"You will get in the car, please," the officer said.

"Hold on a second," Vaughan said. "You have no right to take us anywhere. We're Americans on an important trade mission to your country."

"You will please not make argument with me," the officer said.

Lomonosov interjected, "There is no sense in debating it. You go with him, answer a few questions, then we leave."

The officer-in-charge's tone was not nearly as conciliatory. "You will get into car now!"

Another squad car arrived.

"Mr. Lomonosov is right," I offered. "Debating it with the officer isn't going to get us anywhere. If we run into a problem at police headquarters, we can call the embassy from there."

Fifteen minutes later, we were seated at a scarred wooden table in a stark room I assumed was used for interrogation of prisoners. A female officer with a boxlike body and hair pulled back in a bun so tight it must have been painful, served us tepid tea in paper cups.

"I still don't understand why we're here," Olga

said. "They could have taken our statements at the scene."

"We'll give it another ten minutes," Vaughan said. "If they don't release us by then, I'll call the embassy."

"Where did Mr. Lomonosov go?" I asked.

The door opened and the officer who'd taken us to police headquarters entered the room. He was less stern now, apologizing for detaining us and asking if we wanted more tea.

"What we'd like is to leave," Vaughan said.

"Of course," said the officer. "Now, just a few questions. Tell me what you saw this evening."

"As I told you, we saw nothing," Vaughan replied. "We ducked into the doorway and looked away. We didn't venture back out until the cars were gone."

"Ah, the cars," the officer said. "You will tell me what sort of automobiles they were."

We looked at each other. I said, "I don't think any of us can tell you that. All I know is that one of the vehicles was long and black. I think it was black." To Vaughan: "Was it black?"

"It was a dark color," he said. To Olga: "Did you catch the color?"

She shook her head.

"The men," said the officer. "You will describe them for me?"

"The men on the corner?" Olga said.

"*Nyet*. We know them. They are in the morgue. The men in the cars, with the weapons."

The three of us agreed we didn't have a chance to see any of their faces.

"I told you we saw nothing," Vaughan said. "Bringing us here was a waste of time—*our* time."

The officer shrugged. "It was necessary. It is the way we do things."

"I assume we're free to leave now," I said, standing and straightening my skirt.

"Of course," the officer said, also standing. "I will have someone take you to the Savoy."

"You know where we're staying?" I asked.

"*Da*."

Interesting, I thought. I hadn't mentioned it to him, nor had I heard Vaughan or Olga say it.

The door opened again. Peter Lomonosov, accompanied by Captain Kazakov, my visitor to the hotel suite last night, entered. "*Dobree vecher*, Mrs. Fletcher," Kazakov said.

"Good evening to you," I said. "Is it a coincidence that you just happen to be here?"

"Yes. Coincidence. But now that we are together once again, I offer my apologies for what you have witnessed tonight."

"Who is this?" Olga asked.

I introduced Kazakov to them.

"Ah, your publishing colleagues. It is my pleasure. Unfortunately, what you saw tonight is not unusual these days in Moscow. "Before, it was more peaceful, *da*?" He directed his comment at the other officer.

"What's being done about it?" Vaughan asked.

Kazakov shrugged and displayed a toothy smile. "We try our best but . . . well, it is difficult under the current government. Too much room for corruption. But this is not of interest to you."

"I'd say it is," Vaughan said. "We were subjected to a first-hand glimpse of it tonight."

"For which I can only extend my sympathy," said Kazakov.

"Let's go," Vaughan said.

"A car is waiting outside," Lomonosov said. "I will personally escort you."

A gleaming red unmarked police car stood just outside the front door, its motor running, a young officer at rigid attention by the open rear door.

Kazakov clicked his heels. "A pleasure to meet you, Mr. and Mrs. Buckley. I hope the rest of your stay in Moscow proves to be more pleasant that it has been. *Spakoyni nochi.*"

"Good night," we said in English.

Back at the hotel, Lomonosov offered to buy us a drink. We declined.

"Well, I wish you then a good evening," he said. "A word of advice?"

"Yes?"

"It is not safe for you to walk alone in Moscow these days. Not safe at all, for all visitors. Please do not do it again."

"You don't have to worry about that," Olga said.

The impact of the evening now hit us as we entered the lobby and decided what to do next.

"This trade mission has turned into a nightmare," Olga said.

"Feel up to that talk we were going to have?" I asked Vaughan.

"Sure. Where?"

"Sure you want me along?" Olga asked.

"Absolutely," I said. "Mr. Mulligan at the embassy asked that Vaughan and I not talk about it with others. But since he chose to include Vaughan, I'm sure it wouldn't be a surprise that he discussed it with his wife."

"Actually, I'd just as soon *not* know anything," Olga said.

"Too late for that," Vaughan said. "Besides, Jess hasn't made her decision about whether to go through with it. Maybe among the three of us, we can come to a rational conclusion."

The Savoy Hotel has two bars. Although I was

reluctant to discuss anything of substance in a public place where we might be electronically overheard, I'd come to the conclusion that there probably wasn't a safe place anywhere in Moscow. Discussing it while walking in the street was out of the question, considering what we'd just been through.

"Let's go in that bar," Vaughan suggested, pointing.

"The bar?" I said.

"I can use a drink," Vaughan said. "Besides, all the ambient noise will make it difficult for anyone to hear us."

The bar was busy, and we had to wait a few minutes for a small table to become available. Once we were seated, a pretty young waitress asked, in perfect English, what we wished to drink.

"Vodka," said Vaughan. "Straight."

"Vodka," Olga said. "With tonic."

They looked at me.

"Vodka," I said. "With tomato juice on the side."

Vaughan laughed. "I never thought I'd see the day you'd order a vodka, straight."

"I didn't either. But considering we're in Russia, and considering what we've been through tonight, it seems an appropriate choice."

Forty-five minutes later, we left the bar and waited for the elevator. I hadn't touched my vodka, preferring to sip the tomato juice, which gave Vaughan a second drink without having to order it.

"I still say you shouldn't do it," Olga said as the doors slid open and we stepped inside.

"You're probably right," I said.

"I agree," Vaughan said. The doors closed and we rode to our respective floors.

"Sleep tight," I said as they stepped out into their hallway.

"You, too. See you at breakfast."

The hall was empty as I approached the door to my suite. I inserted my key, opened it, and stepped inside. The tiny red light on my phone was flashing, indicating I had a message. I picked up the receiver and punched in the number connecting me with the hotel's message center.

"You had a call, Mrs. Fletcher, from Ms. Alexandra Kozhina. She called at nine."

"Did she leave a number?"

"No. She said she would call again."

"Thank you."

As I prepared for bed, I suffered a nagging feeling that something wasn't right in the suite. I couldn't identify the source of my unease—just something different.

I went to the piano. The keyboard cover was open. So was the lid covering the inner mechanism. I was certain they'd been closed when I left the room that evening.

I looked elsewhere for signs that someone had been there. Whoever it was hadn't been especially careful, or concerned about covering his, or her, tracks.

I sat by the window and tried to imagine what whoever had been there was looking for. Nothing seemed to have been missing. It took a few minutes before my thoughts went to the note Dimitri Rublev had given me in Washington to pass on to Alexandra Kozhina.

I opened the handbag I'd had with me all evening, returned to the chair, and withdrew the note.

Is this *what they were after?*

I fingered the envelope, turning it over and over in my hands. It was still securely sealed.

Should I open it?

I hate having to make decisions like that.

Chapter Fourteen

I was at breakfast in the hotel dining room with Marge Fargo when the Savoy's concierge sought me out and handed me a telephone message slip: "Ms. Kozhina called. She will call your room again in a half hour."

"A problem?" Marge asked.

"Oh, no," I said. "But I do have to get back to my room for a call. Excuse me."

"You haven't eaten your toast."

"I know. But it's an important call. See you at the meeting at ten."

The moment I arrived in my room I called Vaughan Buckley. Olga answered.

"I'm in my room waiting for Ms. Kozhina to call," I said.

"You've already spoken with her?"

"No. She left a message that she'd be calling back in a half hour."

"Here's Vaughan."

I told him what I'd told Olga.

"I should be there," he said.

"I was hoping you would."

"Olga just got out of bed. She'll join up with us later."

Vaughan arrived five minutes later. I'd ordered coffee and toast from room service, enough for both of us.

"Going through with it?" he asked.

"Yes. I read the note Dimitri Rublev gave me to give to Ms. Kozhina."

His raised eyebrows said precisely what he was thinking.

"I felt I had to, Vaughan, before deciding what to do. It wasn't easy, believe me. But I hate making decisions in the dark, without knowing all the facts."

"Of course. I wasn't being critical. Just surprised, that's all. What did the note say?"

"Read it yourself. I didn't even bother trying to reseal it."

I handed it to him. He put on half-glasses. A puzzled expression crossed his face as he read the short note. He removed his glasses and handed the slip of paper back to me.

I smiled. "Nothing more than a love note," I said.

"So it seems. Mr. Rublev writes nicely. Very poetic."

"A little mawkish for my taste," I said. "But yes, well written. I have another reaction, Vaughan."

"Which is?"

"That those lovely words could contain a code of some sort."

"A code? Not likely."

"Why?"

"Rublev isn't a . . . a spy. He's a writer."

"Can't he be both?"

"I suppose he could."

"We know that Ms. Kozhina is more than a writer."

"We really don't, Jess. All we know is what Mulligan and Karl Warner told us at the embassy."

This time, it was my turn to adopt a skeptical expression.

Vaughan held up a hand. "Okay," he said, "maybe they aren't being truthful. But I think we don't have any choice but to believe what they say about her."

"And if we *do* believe them, then there's every possibility that Rublev, who's obviously quite close to her, might also be involved in what Mulligan and Warner claim she is."

"Still, a code? Let me read it again."

Room service arrived while Vaughan carefully

studied the note. I poured coffee for us and waited for Vaughan to finish. He gave me the note; I, too, gave it a second read.

"Well?" I asked.

"A lover's note, Jess. Sorry, but I don't read anything else into it."

"You're probably right. But there's a look on your face that says you might be thinking what Mulligan thought, that I've been reading too many cold war spy stories. Too active an imagination."

"I wasn't thinking that at all."

"Good. Because that's not what's behind my fast-developing paranoia since this trip began. There's got to be a link between the sudden deaths of Ward Wenington and Vlady Staritova. In both cases it's been said that they didn't die of natural causes. It's also no coincidence that I was chosen to carry a note from Rublev to Alexandra Kozhina. When I returned here last night, I discovered that someone had searched my suite."

"Why didn't you tell me that earlier?"

"I just thought of it."

"I mean, why didn't you call me last night the minute you realized it? You could have been in danger."

"Whoever had been there was long gone by the

time I arrived. I think the person was looking for that note."

"Makes sense. Nothing missing?"

"No. I had the note with me last night. It's always been with me."

"Good. Jess, maybe we should—"

The ringing phone jarred us.

"It's her," I said.

He nodded.

"Use the phone in the bedroom."

"All right."

"As soon as I pick up, do the same."

"Right."

Vaughan stood in the door to the bedroom, the phone in his hand. I picked up the receiver. So did he.

"Hello?"

"Mrs. Fletcher?"

"Yes, Ms. Kozhina. They told me you'd be calling again. Glad we finally connected."

I glanced at Vaughan, who indicated he was on the line.

"I am sorry to have been so . . . how shall I say? . . . so elusive, yes? . . . to be difficult to reach."

"That's quite all right," I said. "I'm glad we finally have this chance to talk. You mentioned you have this mystery writers' group."

"*Da.* Yes."

"And you'd like me to speak to your group."

"Yes. Again, yes."

"Well, I hadn't known about that until you mentioned it, but that shouldn't be a problem. I spoke with an official with our trade mission. He says it will be fine for me to meet with you."

"That is good. Very good news."

"I'm not sure what our schedule is tomorrow—we'll be in Moscow only for another two days. When were you thinking of having me?"

"Tonight? Yes? Once a week we meet. Tonight is our meeting."

I looked to Vaughan. He shrugged. "I believe tonight will be all right, Ms. Kozhina, but I'll have to confirm it. I have your address but not your phone number. I could call you after I clear it and—"

"My phone does not work, Mrs. Fletcher. The system. Something about a central station. I am sorry. I call from a friend's flat."

"May I call you back there?"

"*Nyet.* Perhaps you would be good enough to leave a written message for me."

"All right. Where shall I leave it?"

"At the hotel desk. I will come by at noon. Yes?"

"I should know by then. I'll hear from you about the time and where I'm to go?"

"Yes. I will leave that information at the desk when I find out whether you will come."

"That sounds fine, Ms. Kozhina."

"Please, call me Alexandra."

"And I'm Jessica. I'm sure we'll be seeing each other later. Thank you for calling. Good-bye."

Vaughan hung up in the bedroom and joined me in the living room.

"What do you think?" I asked.

"She sounds . . . well, harmless enough. Hard to believe what Mulligan and Warner say about her."

"I suppose we'd better call Mr. Mulligan. Or is it Warner?"

"I don't know," I said. "I suppose—"

The phone rang. I picked up. "Hello?"

"Mrs. Fletcher. Karl Warner."

"Good morning, Mr. Warner. I was just about to call you."

"Were you? Then I've saved you the trouble. Had breakfast yet?"

I looked at the plate of uneaten toast. "No," I said.

"Be my guest?"

"I—I'm with Mr. Buckley."

"He's invited, too, of course. Say, fifteen minutes. Downstairs? In the restaurant?"

"I'll have to ask him."

"Mrs. Buckley, too, if she wishes to join us."

I held my hand over the mouthpiece and asked Vaughan.

"Sure," he said. "I'll fetch Olga."

"We'll meet you in the restaurant, Mr. Warner. Any special reason for this invitation?"

He laughed. "Just thought we should go over some things before your meeting tonight with Ms. Kozhina. See you in fifteen."

He hung up.

"Why does he want to have breakfast?" Vaughan asked.

"To talk things over before I meet tonight with Ms. Kozhina."

"To talk things over before— How the hell does he know about it? You just hung up on her."

I smiled. "Remember when we were in Washington and you explained all the strange goings-on by saying, 'This is Washington?' "

"Yes."

"Well, this is Moscow. Enough said?"

"The phone."

"The room."

"Everything? *Everywhere?*"

"I certainly hope not."

Chapter Fifteen

Warner was already seated when we arrived at the restaurant. He sprang to his feet and held out chairs for Olga and me.

Once we'd placed our orders, I said, "Mr. Warner, I would really appreciate it if we could be totally honest with one another."

"I wasn't aware we hadn't been, Mrs. Fletcher."

I didn't allow him to get away with that. "You know I've made tentative plans to meet with Ms. Kozhina tonight. You also know that I'm to leave a note for her at the desk, and that she'll leave a note for me with instructions on where and when we're to meet. It's obvious that every word I utter in my suite is heard by people, evidently including you. Now, having said that, let's discuss why you *really* want me to meet with Alexandra Kozhina, and the result you hope will come from that meeting."

Warner listened impassively. When I finished, he said, "Enjoy your breakfast. Then we'll go to some place I *assure* you is secure."

Before leaving the hotel for our ten o'clock meeting, I left a note at the front desk for Alexandra Kozhina advising her that I was free that evening to address her writers' group. I also mentioned that my American publisher, Vaughan Buckley, would accompany me.

Following the meeting, we attended a luncheon hosted by a relatively new newspaper, *Nezavisimaya Gazeta*, founded, we were told, by Yeltsin supporters, but becoming more disillusioned with him and the government with each passing day. At least that's what Pyotr Belopolsky, our Russian host, had said.

A certain sadness about Russia became increasingly obvious the longer we were there. The country had shucked its oppressive Communist yoke, yet was having so much trouble adjusting to suddenly becoming a democracy and free market. There was constant talk of millions of citizens not being paid for months, primarily because the new government hadn't instituted an effective, corruption-free tax collection system, or a legal structure through which wrongs could be righted. And always organized crime lurked behind every business deal, every bank, every government agency. I thought of Ivan, our driver the previous day, who said he had to fork over a large percentage of his income to mobsters, or else his car, and undoubtedly himself, was in physical jeopardy. I found myself saying a silent prayer that the people of this vast country would find a way to prosper in peace, not only for their sake, but for the rest of the world as well.

After lunch Vaughan, Olga, and I swung by the Savoy to check whether Ms. Kozhina had picked up my note and left one for me. She had. Her message said: "I am pleased you will speak to us tonight. The meeting is at eight o'clock. A car and driver will pick you and Mr. Buckley up at quarter before eight at front of hotel. Thank you. A. Kozhina."

"I still say there's something wrong with all of this," Olga said after reading the note.

"Maybe there is," her husband said. "We'll find out soon enough."

"And you're adamant about my not going with you," she said.

"That's right."

"But you didn't hesitate ringing me in on everything leading up to it."

"Because I didn't think it would amount to anything. Just a fascinating bit of intrigue for us to share," Vaughan said. "But now that Jess is going through with it, I insist you stay here at the hotel."

His laugh was a little forced. "It will all probably end up a big nothing. All Jess has to do is make an offer to this mysterious Kozhinà lady, get her reaction, and report it back to Warner. Hardly the sort of clandestine mission likely to get anyone hurt."

"Then I should be able to go with you," Olga said.

"She's right," I offered.

"Jess. I—"

"Of course I'm right," said Olga. "Besides, why should you two have all the fun? I'd love to attend a Russian writers' meeting, see how they think, what they're up to. The next Pushkin or Chekhov or Tolstoy might be there."

"Unlikely," Vaughan said, resignation in his voice.

"Then it's settled," Olga said. She looked at her watch. "Time to get to the afternoon meeting." She smiled sweetly at Vaughan. "I never knew the publishing business was so much fun."

That afternoon's gathering was not what I would term "fun." A panel of Russian publishers—we were told there were an estimated three thousand independent publishers in Russia; the panel represented the few who were solvent—droned on about their business woes, some speaking in fractured English, others filtering their remarks through a translator. Their ultimate message was clear enough, no matter in what language it was presented. They wanted American publishers to buy their way into the Russian book market through partnerships forged with the Russians.

"At the profit margin we operate under, the last thing Buckley House needs is a Russian partner tottering on the brink of bankruptcy," Vaughan whispered to me. "And with the Russian mob as a not very silent partner."

I chuckled. I was thinking the same thing. I was also pondering how lucky I was to not be in business, with all its intrigue and pressures and perpetual eye on the bottom line. Running my own little, one-person writing factory was quite enough, thank you.

The ubiquitous cocktail party followed the meeting, with caviar and smoked salmon and an unending supply of vodka. I wasn't surprised to see the ever-present Karl Warner at the party. But the arrival of Tom Mulligan of the American Embassy was unexpected. He came directly to where I chatted with a group of Russians, one of whom made an enthusiastic pitch for the rights to my books. "Poor Vlady," the Russian said. "He would have been a good publisher for you, Mrs. Fletcher. But, alas, poor Vlady is no longer with us, which means there is no one at his publishing house to do your works justice. I, on the other hand, have a fine staff who would—"

"Mr. Mulligan," I said, happy for the intrusion. "How nice to see you again."

The Russian publishers drifted away, leaving Mulligan and me alone.

"Learning a lot about your Russian colleagues?" he asked.

"Oh, yes. This has been a fascinating, as well as informative experience."

"Glad to hear it."

I looked past him to where Warner stood with a small cluster of people. Although he was engaged in conversation with them, I had no doubt his attention was on us.

"Have a pleasant evening planned?" Mulligan asked.

I wasn't sure how to answer. Did he know about my date to address Alexandra Kozhina's writers' group? Probably. On the other hand, maybe he wasn't in Warner's loop. We'd been told at lunch that the performance of the LenKom Theater and the Russian nightclub visit, both having been cancelled due to Vlady Staritova's death, had been rescheduled for that evening. Was Mulligan referring to those plans?

I replied to his question in my best noncommittal, bureaucratic, governmental manner: "Yes," I said.

He gave me a wide smile. "Good. I want to be

sure our distinguished American visitors enjoy themselves. Hope to see you again before you leave, Mrs. Fletcher. And thank you again for signing the books for me and my wife. Much appreciated."

He sauntered away, his walk that of a man sure of himself in any situation.

His departure left me looking directly at Warner, who also smiled, nodded in a way that said everything would be fine, and left the room.

"Dinner plans?" Marge Fargo asked, coming up behind me.

"Ah, no. Well, yes, actually. I promised some people we'd get together tonight." Which I had done, although it didn't involve dinner. The whitest of lies.

"Oh, sorry," she said. "I was hoping to catch some quiet time with you during the trip. Happy with Buckley House?"

Her question caught me off-guard. "Pardon?" I said.

"Are you happy with Buckley House publishing your books?"

"Why, yes."

"Good to hear. You know, Jess, sometimes even the best of relationships in this business run their course. A staleness sets in. I've just established a new division devoted exclusively to murder mysteries.

You'd be the crown jewel of that division. Plenty of money to put behind your books."

A wave of pervasive discomfort swept over me. I didn't know Marge Fargo very well, hardly at all, actually, aside from her reputation in the publishing world, which was a fine one. Here I was being wooed away from my publisher of many years, Buckley House, not the biggest in the business but one of the most respected. I'd developed a strong friendship with Vaughan Buckley and had always been blissfully pleased with the job he did publishing and marketing my books. It was an awkward situation Marge Fargo was putting me in, one I was anxious to escape.

"Your new division sounds exciting," I said. "You'll have to tell me more about it one day. Maybe on the flight home. But Buckley House and I are—well, we've become inseparable, in a sense."

"I understand," she said. "Vaughan is one of the best. Still, change can sometimes be beneficial for an author. Let's talk about it at another time. Going to the theater and nightclub?"

"I don't think so, Marge. Dinner with these friends, then early to bed. I'm beat."

"Just a few more days to go. See you later."

My dinner plans had been decided earlier that afternoon. Vaughan suggested we have room service for the three of us sent to my suite. That would give us a chance to discuss the evening ahead, and to be at the hotel when the car sent by Ms. Kozhina arrived. I found it somewhat strange that a writers' group, in any country, would have the resources to send a car for someone. Then again, I suppose I should have been flattered they thought so much of my appearance that they extended that courtesy. Probably one of the group's members, not a hired car.

On the other hand, what if it wasn't a writer's group? What if it was as Warner and Mulligan claimed, a subversive Communist cell with an important role to play in attempting to overthrow the Yeltsin government?

I preferred to not think about that.

Chapter Sixteen

We ordered up steaks and salads, and a platter of cookies for dessert. While waiting for room service to arrive, Vaughan and Olga insisted I show off my musical training by playing a few tunes on the piano. They didn't believe my protestations about how musically inept I was—until I'd fumbled through a simple song or two. They were polite in their praise, but I knew they were pleased when the knock came at the door announcing dinner was about to be served, and that the concert was over.

It was pleasurable dining privately with my two good friends in the opulence of my suite. The subject of what we'd be doing later that evening didn't come up until I'd poured coffee and had passed around the platter of tiny Russian sweets.

"Want to go over what you're supposed to say?" Vaughan asked.

"I've done that a thousand times in my head," I said. "It seems so simple, but—"

"What you're concerned about is her reaction, I presume," he said.

"Yes. I also wonder how I'm going to find time alone with her, at least enough to have a one-on-one conversation."

"Maybe we can help with that," Olga said. "You know, divert the attention of others away from you and this Ms. Kozhina."

"We'll look for an opportunity to do that," said Vaughan.

"Time to get downstairs," I said. "The car will be here in ten minutes."

"How do I look?" Olga asked, standing and extending her arms.

Vaughan laughed and said, "You look like one of James Bonds's girls."

"Is that a compliment?" Olga asked.

"Decidedly so," he said.

"Let's go," I said. "Musn't keep my Russian writers' group waiting."

"But we're all agreed on one thing," Vaughan said. "If any of us smells trouble, we're out of there, no questions asked."

"You'd think Mr. Warner and whoever he works for would have arranged for a way for us to get in touch with them in an emergency," Olga said as he went to the door.

"Maybe he has," I said, opening the door. Outside in the hall was the same man who'd been stationed there at various times since our arrival.

"*Dobry vecher*," I said, pleasantly.

"*Dobry vecher*," he mumbled, turning away.

"Who's he?" Vaughan asked when we were out of earshot.

"Don't know his name," I said. "Sort of an anonymous companion."

"Gives me the creeps," Olga said as the elevator doors opened.

"Him?" I said.

"This whole place. The hotel, the city, everything."

"Let's not overreact," Vaughan said, stepping aside for us to enter.

We rode down in silence.

The Savoy's large lobby was a beehive of activity when we came off the elevator. That it was a center of international business travel was evidenced by the mix of nationalities milling about and speaking different languages, but undoubtedly all there for the same reason—to explore ways to profit from the new Russia.

We went to the door leading to the street, where

the busy sidewalk mirrored what was going on inside.

"Do we know what car to look for?" Olga asked.

"No," I said, standing on tiptoe to see over the throng of people blocking my view. There were a number of hired cars with drivers waiting for whomever they were assigned to drive that night.

"Maybe we should go back inside and call someone," Vaughan suggested.

"Call *who*?" I asked. "I don't have Ms. Kozhina's number."

"Mrs. Fletcher!"

We turned to see a young man making his way through the crowd in our direction, hand held high. "Mrs. Fletcher!"

"Yes," I said.

"I . . . am . . . driver," he said, breathless. He wore a black suit and black cap with a small brim. Long strands of silky blond hair sprouted out on all sides.

"I'm glad you found us," I said.

He looked at me quizzically.

"*Gavareete lee vy pa angleeskee?*" I asked.

"*Nyet.* No . . . speak . . . much . . . ah . . . *angleeskee.*"

"That's fine," Vaughan said. "Where's your car? Automobile."

His face lit up. "Ah, yes. Come."

We followed him along the sidewalk and to a side street where he'd parked his car, a long, sleek gray limousine. So much for one of the writers' group's members picking us up. Either Alexandra Kozhina and her group had lots of money, or the driver was someone's relative.

He opened one of the rear doors and allowed us to enter, closed the door, and ran around to the driver's side where he slid behind the wheel.

"What is your name?" Vaughan asked.

The driver turned. "Name? Ah, yes. Misha. My . . . name . . . is . . . Misha."

"Good," Vaughan said. "Where are we going?"

Misha's answer was to start the engine, slip the limo into gear, and pull into traffic on the main street, oblivious to other vehicles in his way.

"Hang on," Vaughan said.

His warning was justified. Misha drove like a madman, cutting off cars and trucks and large red buses, one hand on the wheel, the other pressed firmly against the horn button.

"Would you please slow down," I said, trying to penetrate the glass partition he'd closed between him and the passenger compartment.

"Save your breath," Olga said, grabbing her husband's arm as we took a corner without slowing.

I tried to gain a sense of the direction in which we

were going, but it was difficult because of our speed, and the darkened windows in the limo. Besides, since I didn't know the city, there weren't any reference points to use.

After fifteen minutes, I started to become concerned. Dimitri Rublev had said the section of Moscow in which Alexandra Kozhina lived, Kitay Gorod, was close to the Kremlin, and I knew that the Kremlin was within walking distance of the hotel.

I knocked on the partition. Misha cocked his head. I looked for a handle that would allow me to slide the partition open, but there wasn't any.

"Open it!" Vaughan yelled.

Misha answered by making a hard right and screeching to a halt in front of a nondescript building, in a row of nondescript buildings. He hopped from the limo, came around, and opened the door for us. Vaughan was closest to the door; Olga sat between Vaughan and me, leaving me as the last person who would exit.

Vaughan got out and stretched.

Olga looked at me and said, "God, what a ride. He's a madman."

"I know," I said, drawing a deep breath of relief that we'd finally—and safely—reached our destination.

"Is this where she lives?" Olga asked.

"I don't know," I said.

"Come on," Vaughan urged from the sidewalk.

Olga slowly slid across the broad seat and accepted Vaughan's offer of his hand. It was at that moment I noticed someone slip behind the wheel. It wasn't Misha, no blond curls protruding from beneath his cap. It was someone else.

I turned to see Vaughan about to extend his hand to me.

Then, someone came up and pushed Vaughan aside.

The door slammed shut.

The *click* of the electronic door locks reverberated throughout the rear passenger compartment.

I heard Vaughan yell, "Jess!"

The driver rammed the accelerator to the floor, sending me back hard against the seat.

I pivoted and looked out the rear window. Vaughan and Olga stood helplessly by, flanked by two tough-looking men.

I swung around, leaned forward, and pounded my fist on the partition. The driver turned his head slightly.

It was Ivan, our driver of the day before.

I don't swear. But if I'd known a four-letter word in Russian, I certainly would have used it.

Chapter Seventeen

Street signs blurred as we raced past them. I tried to open the lock on the nearest door but couldn't. My mind ran as fast as the limo, conflicting thoughts and fears bumping into each other, anger coming to the fore one moment, replaced by heart-pounding fear the next. Most prevailing was the sense of hopelessness, of impotency. There was nothing I could do except wait until we got to where we were going and see what that situation brought.

I thought of movies I'd seen in which a kidnap victim has the presence of mind to observe landmarks to be used later when the abductors are brought to justice and put on trial. I would have tried to do that, too, except the combination of night, and the darkened windows, made it impossible to get a fix on anything. I did sense one thing, however. We were leaving the city proper and heading into a less populated area. That was even more frightening.

Was I being taken to some remote location to be killed? Why would anyone want to kill me? What had I done? As far as I knew, my only action was to agree to deliver a lover's note to a young Russian woman who also happened to be a writer. Was Vaughan Buckley right, that the note contained some sort of code? Even if it did, I hadn't written it, nor could I know what it meant.

And why would I be kidnapped? The only contact I'd had with this Alexandra Kozhina was a few telephone conversations.

But as I continued to chew on these thoughts, it became more evident that the complication had been injected by my own people, my own government. Here I was agreeing to deliver a message to Ms. Kozhina on behalf of those same people and that same government. That had removed me from the simple role of, as the travel book publisher had said during our flight to Moscow, a "courier of romance." I knew one thing: Assuming I got out of this alive, I'd leave playing Cupid to others more constitutionally suited for that dangerous occupation.

I was mired deep in thought and fear when Ivan pulled off onto a narrow dirt road that was deeply rutted. I strained to see where we were; all I saw were the silhouettes of trees against a bright night-time sky. Ivan stopped the limo, got out, and stood in front of it. He lit a cigarette and continued to stand there, the smoke visibly wafting up into the air each time he took a puff.

I tried the door. It was locked.

I heard voices. A moment later, the shadows of two people fell across my window as they passed. An animated conversation in Russian erupted between the newcomers and Ivan. Then the door was opened, and the beam of a flashlight blinded me. My hands reflexively came up to shield my eyes.

"Out!" a man said in English.

"Get the light out of my eyes," I said.

"Out!" he repeated.

I slid across the leather seat and paused at the open door. The flashlight was now trained on the second man who'd arrived, young, tall, and with a long, chiseled face.

"Who are you?" I asked, leaving the vehicle and planting my feet on the spongy soil.

"You will, please, come with us," the man holding the flashlight said.

"I demand to know why I've been abducted," I said, surprised at the resolve in my voice. My inner trembling was unstated.

"Please, not to argue with me," he said. He touched my elbow.

"Keep your hands off me," I said, following him around the car to where another vehicle was parked beneath a clump of low-hanging trees. Its lights were off, the full moon's glow providing natural illumination.

The man led me to the second vehicle, a small sedan, and opened the rear door.

"I am not getting in there" I said.

"You will, please, not to argue with me."

"Don't argue with you? I am an American citizen. I have been kidnapped. I insist upon speaking with my embassy."

The man's fleshy lips parted in a smile. He bowed slightly, extended his hand toward the open door, and said, "No trouble for you, lady, if you . . . do not give me trouble, huh?"

I turned. Ivan and the other man had come up behind me. Obviously, there was nothing physical I could do against them. My feeble verbal demands probably had no greater effect than to amuse them. My only chance, I decided, was to go along with whatever they wanted, and hope to find an opportunity to escape somewhere along the line.

"All right," I said, climbing into the smaller vehicle. The door slammed behind me, and the two men who'd just arrived got in the front, leaving Ivan standing alone. I'd felt sorry for that young man and his tale of being taken advantage of by Russia's mob. Wasted pity, I thought as the car's engine roared to life, the lights came on, and we headed back in the direction from which we'd come, along the rutted dirt road to the larger roadway, and then back toward Moscow. Soon the lights of the city came into view. Not long after that, we drove down a wide boulevard, turned off onto a smaller street, pulled into a courtyard, and stopped at the front door of a pretty redbrick building.

"Do you mind if I ask where we are?" I asked.

"Moscow," the man in the front passenger seat said, chuckling. I didn't break a smile; it wasn't funny to me.

My door was opened, and the two men escorted me into a small foyer, where one of them pressed a button that sounded a faint buzz from somewhere inside. He didn't give it a single push. Instead, he seemed to tap out a code—two short bursts, a prolonged buzz, then three short ones. A metallic clang signaled that the interior door had been released. One of the men opened it, and we stepped into a larger space with a staircase.

"Up!" I was told.

I slowly climbed the stairs, one of my captors in

front of me, one behind. Three flights up, the man ahead of me went to a door and knocked, using his knuckles to tap out the same code he'd used downstairs. The door opened just far enough to extend the security chain.

The man said something in Russian.

A woman's voice replied.

The chain was released, and the door opened all the way. The men stepped back to allow me to enter. Facing me from inside the apartment was a slender young woman with loose blond hair framing a nicely sculptured face. She wore tight black leather pants slung low on her hips, black high heels with a painted toenail protruding through an opening in front of each shoe, and a form-fitting yellow sweater that stopped short of covering her belly button. She was without makeup.

"Mrs. Fletcher," she said.

"Ms. Kozhina," I said.

"Welcome. Please come in. We have much to talk about."

Chapter Eighteen

The door closed behind me; the men evidently weren't invited to the party.

"Please, come in," Alexandra said, gesturing toward the living room.

I hesitated. I was still shaken—and angry—at what had just happened.

"I am sorry for the way you have come here, but it was necessary. Please."

The living room was spacious and nicely decorated. The wallpaper was a delicate yellow with tiny white flowers. Two large oval Oriental rugs covered a burnished wood floor. The art on the walls was contemporary. A fire smoldered in a fireplace surrounded by floor-to-ceiling bookcases.

The furniture was old, the sort I would have expected to see in an Early American Maine farmhouse. A large wooden desk with a herringbone inlay stood in front of a heavily draped window. Chairs on either side of it were decidedly Hepplewhite. A massive breakfront sideboard held a dozen flickering candles in silver candlesticks of various heights. Soft classical music came from unseen speakers.

"Sit, please," she said, indicating the other dominant piece of furniture in the room, an early Victorian sofa upholstered in heavy red-and-yellow raised fabric.

I decided to go with the flow, as the saying goes. I didn't have any choice. After I was seated, she asked, "Vodka? Wine—red? white? Or maybe a soft drink. Coca-Cola? Tea?"

"Tea would be fine."

"One moment, please."

She disappeared through a door leading, I assumed, to the kitchen, leaving me alone.

Was there a way out?

The men undoubtedly waited in the hallway.

I got up and parted the drapes. There were windows, but no fire escape. Besides, although I try to keep myself in fairly good shape, I wasn't keen on making that sort of dramatic escape.

Thoughts of bolting were purely academic, however, because Ms. Kozhina reappeared carrying a tray on which a teapot, a single cup, and sugar and cream rested. She placed it on the desk.

"That was quick," I said.

"I had already made it," she said. "I thought you might be a tea drinker."

"Your English is better in person than on the phone," I said.

She smiled. "It is sometimes better for people to not know how well you speak their language."

"Oh? Better in what way?"

She replied by pouring tea into my cup. "Cream? Sugar?"

"Neither, thank you."

She handed the cup to me, poured herself a glass of vodka, sat next to me on the couch, kicked off her shoes, and tucked her bare feet beneath her. She raised her glass. "To the pleasure of meeting the famous Jessica Fletcher."

The gesture took me aback. It was as though I'd been invited to a party by a friend of long standing, a social event. In reality, I'd been tricked into meeting her, and was physically abducted on her behalf.

I did not return the toast. Instead, I said, "Your writers' group seems to be running late."

"There is such a group, you know," she said, sipping.

"But it isn't meeting tonight."

"No. That was what you call . . . a white lie, yes?"

"A bigger lie than that, Ms. Kozhina."

We said nothing to each other for a minute. I used that silent time to more closely observe her. She was a beautiful young woman. Her face, especially her green eyes, exuded sensuality and intelligence. At the same time, there was a lurking cunning that was off-putting.

I broke the silence. "Why was it necessary to forcibly bring me here, switch cars so that we couldn't be followed? Why didn't you simply invite me to your apartment—for tea?"

She sighed, got up, and refilled her glass. "Mrs. Fletcher, you come from a country in which things are taken for granted. It is not so here in Russia."

"I thought you enjoy more freedom now than when you were a Communist country."

"On paper, yes. But there are those who would like to see us go back to that Communist system."

Like you.

"You have the note Dimitri sent?" she asked.

"Yes. I should tell you that I read it."

"I know."

"You do?"

"Yes. Perhaps if you had not, your treatment this night would not have been necessary."

"I'm not sure I follow. What's wrong with having read a lover's note, aside from the impropriety of it?"

Her mouth formed into a small smile. "The note, please."

I opened my handbag, removed the envelope, and handed it to her. She read the note, her lips silently forming the words. When she had finished, she lowered the note to her lap, turned to me, and said, "Unfortunate."

"What's unfortunate?"

"That someone like you should be asked to carry this to me."

"It made sense at the time," I said. "Your friend, Mr. Rublev, said you were a writer who enjoyed my books. Since I was coming to Russia on a trade mission, it was logical for me to look you up and deliver the note. Now, of course, I realize I should have told your friend to find another messenger service."

She went to the window and peeped through the drapes. Turning, she said, "It is time to go."

"Go where?"

"You will see when we get there."

"Ms. Kozhina, I don't intend to move from this couch until I have some answers."

"In due time."

"No. 'Due time' is now. *Right* now."

She sighed and said, "You wish to deliver to me the message from your officials."

I suppose shock was written all over my face because she followed up with, "Do not be surprised at the things we know, Mrs. Fletcher. There are no secrets in Russia. Only confusion about what to do with what we know."

"Since you already know what I was supposed to convey to you," I said, "allow me to say it."

"Then be quick. We must leave."

"My government—"

No, I thought. I musn't talk as though I were functioning in some official capacity. I started over.

"Ms. Kozhina, as you know, I am a writer. I'm not affiliated with any government organization. My only intention was to deliver a note to you from a friend, and to give a talk to your writers' group. When some officials involved with the trade mission learned that I had planned to see you, they asked me to deliver another message, quite different and aside from what's contained in the note."

She listened impassively, leaning against her desk, arms folded across her chest, eyes trained on me.

"I've been told that you are an important figure in the Communist movement to overthrow the democratic government of President Yeltsin. I've been told that there is the possibility that you might consider betraying your group by providing information from inside it to—I don't know who would receive that information. Someone in my government perhaps.

Someone in President Yeltsin's government. It doesn't matter to me. Because you are supposedly an admirer of mine, they—whoever they are—felt you might be more inclined to listen to me than to one of their own."

She said nothing.

"I was told to say to you that there are many ways you would be compensated. I don't know what they are, but I was assured—and I am to assure you—that they will make it worth your while to cooperate with them."

When she continued to maintain her silence, I added, "But since you knew what it was I intended to say, you've undoubtedly already made up your mind whether to accept their offer."

"I would offer more tea, but there is not time."

"I don't care about tea, Ms. Kozhina. You refuse to respond to what I've said?"

"Mrs. Fletcher, you simply do not understand what is at stake here. Please, we must go."

"I'm going nowhere," I said, hoping my voice reflected conviction.

"One thing I did not think you were, Mrs. Fletcher, was a foolish woman. I can call them." She pointed to the door.

I drew a deep breath and said, "There is no reason for me to go with you. I know nothing more than what I've already said. I've delivered the message. Your response to it doesn't concern me. I also remind you, Ms. Kozhina, that I am here as an official guest of the Russian and American governments. I'm sure the friends I was with when your people so rudely abducted me have gone to the authorities, and that a manhunt is already under way."

Provided, of course, that Vaughan and Olga hadn't been detained, too.

She ignored my warning, slipped on a powder blue windbreaker with LOS ANGELES DODGERS emblazoned across the back, and went to the door. She turned, a hand on her hip. "Your choice, Mrs. Fletcher. A pleasant trip to our next destination—or an unpleasant one."

Her logic wasn't lost on me. I reluctantly stood, took a final look around her living room, and followed her into the hallway, where the two men lounged against the wall. We looked at each other; more accurately, I glared at them. We walked past them, down the stairs, and out to the courtyard. The smaller car in which I'd been brought to the building wasn't there. Instead, the limo driven by Ivan stood at the ready.

We entered the passenger compartment. To my surprise, the men did not join us.

My heart tripped. Aside from Ivan, I was now

alone with Alexandra Kozhina. I knew I could never have overcome the two men. But the odds had evened a little. Two women. Granted, she was considerably younger. But with a combination of luck, prudent thinking, and determination, I could possibly extricate myself from the situation. The key was to stay alert to any opportunity.

Ms. Kozhina spent the first few minutes peering through the limo's darkened glass. I could see that we were moving into a busy part of Moscow, and strained to identify landmarks. It wasn't long before I saw the lights of the Hotel Savoy, my hotel. Were we going there?

We passed it.

The Kremlin was the next familiar sight; we passed that, too.

"Do you mind telling me where we're going?" I asked, not expecting an answer.

"My apartment," Alexandra said.

"Didn't we just leave your apartment?"

"No. That was a . . . How do you say it? . . . a safe house."

A safe house.

Where spies congregate.

Shades of John le Carré and Eric Ambler.

All those spy novels I did read.

We came to a stop in front of a low building, a

shop of sorts on the ground floor—I didn't know what sort of shop it was because I couldn't translate the Russian sign. Ms. Kozhina led me from the limo, while Ivan stayed behind the wheel.

Was this my chance to bolt?

Alexandra looked at me as though she knew exactly what I was thinking. I heard the limo door shut. Ivan now stood next to me.

Since leaving the so-called safe house, fear had been mitigated by curiosity. I'm a naturally curious person, which I suppose all writers are, for better or for worse. It's usually held me in good stead, although there have been times—and my good friend, Dr. Seth Hazlitt, often chides me for it—that my curiosity has led me into trouble.

I'd agreed to deliver the note to Alexandra Kozhina from Dimitri Rublev because I was curious to meet a Russian writer on a personal basis, outside the official structure of the trade mission.

Curiosity was what led me to agree to deliver a clandestine message to Ms. Kozhina on behalf of certain officials of my government. How else could I explain my decision?

Now, standing in front of Ms. Kozhina's apartment building, I was—yes, cursedly—*curious* to see what was next.

Alexandra opened a door next to the shop,

exposing a short flight of stairs. At the top was a landing on which four doors faced. She inserted a key in one, opened it, and said, "Please. Come in."

Her apartment was considerably smaller and less handsomely furnished than the safe house. It consisted of one main room, off which there was a Pullman kitchen, and an open door leading to a cubicle of a bathroom. One window allowed the intermittent flash of neon from outside to provide bursts of light in the room.

I took the only chair in the room while she punched a button on an answering machine. The deep, gruff voice of a man speaking Russian came through the tiny speaker. Alexandra listened impassively.

The next man on the incoming message tape spoke English. "Your eyes are like stars in the night."

She glanced at me.

Where had I heard that line before?

Of course. It was one of many terms of endearment written in the note to her from Dimitri Rublev.

I also had the nagging feeling that I recognized the second caller's voice. But I couldn't put a name to it. All I knew was that I'd heard it before.

Hearing that second recorded message visibly changed Alexandra Kozhina. Until that moment, she'd been a self-possessed, calm, icy young woman.

But those words—"Your eyes are like stars in the night"—unnerved her. It was as though all the air came out of her. She slumped back against the table, closed her eyes, and drew her mouth into a thin, hard line.

"Are you all right?" I asked.

She opened her eyes. "What?" she said.

"Are you all right? That message seemed to have upset you."

"Yes, I'm fine. Just fine."

"The second caller said something that was in the note from Mr. Rublev," I said.

She lowered her head and exhaled loudly. Then, slowly, quietly, she began to weep. I went to her and placed a hand on her slender shoulder. "What is it?" I asked. "What's going on?"

She looked up at me, fighting against the tears, and said, "There has been a change."

"A change from what? Please, Ms. Kozhina, I realize I'm not in a position to make demands. But surely, out of simple courtesy—out of compassion—you owe me some sort of explanation."

She wiped her eyes with the back of her hand, looked at me, a softer expression on her pretty face, and said, "You are right, of course. I owe you an apology."

My spirits lifted. Maybe this nightmare was about to end.

"But we must leave—now!"

"You'll get no argument from me."

"No, you misunderstand. We must leave before they come."

"Before *who* come?"

"The men who will kill us."

My elevated spirits of a moment ago came crashing down.

"Who are these men?" I asked. "Why would they want to kill you? Kill *me*?"

"No time to explain. Come!"

I assumed we would return to the front of the building, where Ivan waited with the limo. Instead, we left the apartment—Ms. Kozhina didn't even bother to close the door behind us—and went up the flight of stairs until reaching a heavy metal door leading to the roof.

"Why are we up here?" I asked, catching my breath as we stepped out onto the flat roof.

Her answer was to place her index finger to her lips and to slip a heavy bar down into a slot to lock the door from the outside.

I looked up into the Moscow sky. The air was heavy, the way it is back home in Cabot Cove when a storm is coming. But the smell was different, very different. I suppose that's because we were in a city, rather than the open spaces of Maine and its fragrance of pine trees and flowers and the salty sea. There was also the odor of fear.

My fear.

I was more frightened at that moment than I could ever remember being. Nothing made sense to me. I was in a strange country that had been, until only a few years ago, committed to bombing the United States into oblivion. I'd found a body in Washington, a man who'd taken me to lunch that very day and asked me to report back any conversations I had with Russian officials. My Russian publisher dropped dead at a dinner we'd attended. I was told neither death resulted from natural causes.

An official of the American Embassy in Moscow asked me to carry a message to an alleged Communist sympathizer, asking her to become a double agent.

Which I'd done, proudly, and blindly.

And now here I was on a rooftop in Moscow, with a beautiful young woman who bolts at hearing a sloppy, adoring message on her answering machine, and who informs me there are men wanting to kill us.

The next time I'm invited on a trade mission for

the United States, I'll be busy, I decided as I followed her to the edge of the roof.

"What are we doing?" I asked.

"Going down," she replied, slinging a leg over the edge and planting her foot on the top rung of a metal ladder.

"Not me," I said.

The hard expression on her face returned. "Don't be a fool," she said. "It's the only way to escape them."

"Escape *who*?"

"Come. It is not far."

She disappeared.

I peered over the roof's edge. She was halfway down. She stopped her descent, looked up, and said, "Follow! I will explain when we are safe."

I turned and looked at the metal door through which we'd come. Did I hear footsteps? The next sound was that of someone trying to open the door from inside.

I looked down again to where Alexandra now stood in an alley behind the building. She waved for me to follow.

The noise from the other side of the door became louder, fists banging on it.

I drew a deep breath, slowly placed one leg over the edge, found the top rung, maneuvered the rest of my body over, and slowly started down, heart pounding, eyes closed. "Just take it slow," I said aloud to myself, "one step at a time. One foot, then the other. That's right. Nothing to worry about. You'll reach the bottom and—"

Men's voices at the top of the ladder caused me to look up. My foot slipped off the rung, and I slid down the rest of the way, not a great distance, but far enough for me to land feet first with an impact that sent a jolt of pain up my legs.

Ms. Kozhina grabbed my hand and pulled me to where the alley opened on to a street. "Please, faster," she said, pulling me along with her.

A yellow taxi with a checkered band on the door indicating it was an official cab, and a green light in the corner of the windshield announcing it was available, stood at the curb. Alexandra opened the door, pushed me past it, and scrambled in beside me.

"This is insane," I managed to say as she shouted something at the driver in Russian. We roared away from the curb.

"I am sorry to be so rough," Alexandra said, "but it is a matter of life or death."

"You'd said you'd explain," I said.

"Yes. Later. When we are safe."

"We'll be safe if we go directly to the American Embassy."

There wasn't time for her to reply because after traveling only two blocks, the driver brought the taxi to a jarring halt. Alexandra threw rubles at him, opened the door, and dragged me out. A large red neon letter M announced we were at an entrance to the famed, efficient Moscow Metro.

We looked at each other. This was it, I thought, my chance to get away. All I had to do was take off at a run in any direction, hopefully losing myself in the crowds of people on the street.

Alexandra knew what I was thinking. She narrowed her eyes, placed both hands on my arms, and said, "You are not safe, Mrs. Fletcher, unless you come with me. Soon, it will be over. Okay?"

We went down into the underground station and boarded a crowded train that had just pulled in.

"Where are we going?" I asked, adrenaline flowing, a thin film of perspiration on my forehead and upper lip.

"To be with friends," she said in a stage whisper.

The ride seemed interminable. But we eventually reached our destination, a stop called *Shchkinskaya*. We climbed the stairs to street level. Alexandra paused, as though to get her bearings. A beggar without legs sat on the sidewalk. He held out a plate. A small battery-powered radio was next to him. Although I couldn't understand what the announcer said, it sounded like a newscast.

"They are looking for you," Alexandra said.

"Who?"

"The police."

She started to walk away from the beggar, but I grabbed her arm. "What else are they saying?"

She leaned closer to the radio. "Your friends are safe."

"Vaughan and Olga?"

"They reported your kidnapping." She listened for another few seconds. "The police say you were abducted by either Communists or the *mafiya*."

She looked at me.

"Which is it?" I asked.

"Come," she said, grabbing my hand.

I pulled free and dropped rubles on the beggar's plate.

"He'll just buy vodka," she said, again taking my hand and leading me around the corner in the direction of what looked like an industrial area. The hustle-bustle at the top of the Metro stairs gradually gave way to a dark, narrow street lined with warehouses. We walked quickly, Alexandra setting the pace, and crossed the street to where a single storefront broke up the gray monotony of the industrial buildings. Yellow light from deep inside reached the front window, casting a gentle glow over carved wooden figures.

Alexandra rapped on the door. When no one responded, she knocked again, louder this time. A door to the rear of the shop opened, allowing more light to spill into the shop itself. A man stood in the open doorway. He was small and hunched over. Because the light source was behind him, I saw him only in silhouette.

"Who is he?" I asked.

"Sssssh."

The man approached the front door with the sort of shuffle common in older people, unsure of his steps and not wanting to fall. As he peered through the door's glass, I could see that his face was as old as his gait. Errant strands of hair rose straight up from a bald pate. His glasses were thick, magnifying his eyes behind them.

"Alexandra?" he said loud enough for us to hear through the door.

"*Da,*" she said. "Open up."

Unlocking the door and fumbling with interior security chains was a tortuous process. Finally, the door swung open and he stepped outside, looked left and right, then led us inside.

His interest was very much on me.

Alexandra spoke in Russian, then said to me in

English, "He wanted to know who you were. I told him you are my friend."

I wasn't sure how to respond. I was there only because I'd been duped by her. I'd been thrown into cars, forced to climb down from a roof on a metal ladder, and was told there were men wanting to kill me. *My friend?* If that were true, our friendship was bizarre enough to be worthy of a daytime TV talk show.

He looked at me with cocked head and narrowed eyes behind the twin circles of bottle glass resting on his nose. I understood when he asked Alexandra whether I spoke Russian.

"*Nyet*," she replied.

"No," I said.

He managed a small smile, pleased that I'd understood his question.

The little old man slowly led us to his office at the rear of the shop. As we moved, we passed framed art on the walls.

"Is this a gallery?" I asked Alexandra in a lowered voice reserved for galleries and museums.

"Yes," she said.

The office was testimony to chaos and clutter. Narrow aisles between waist-high mounds of books and newspapers afforded the only passage. Two small windows were covered with heavily taped cardboard. The desk was obscured by piles of papers, unframed artwork, and books, many of them very old, judging from the musty odor.

"His name is Josef," Alexandra said. "He is my friend."

"Fine," I said. "But why are we here?"

"To save our lives. You will excuse me, please. Josef and I must discuss things. Be patient."

They disappeared into the shop area, leaving me alone in the office and again facing the decision whether to attempt to escape, or to trust Alexandra Kozhina. I opted for the latter. I didn't know where in Moscow I was at the moment. To venture out into the street seemed foolhardy—providing I could. What would I do once I was out? Find a Russian policeman? I didn't speak the language. Besides, could I trust a Russian policeman? Could I trust *anyone*?

I'm always disappointed at movies in which the hero or heroine does something dumb, something everyone in the audience wouldn't do if placed in a similar situation.

If this were a movie, would the audience think I was dumb for not running for my life?

Or would it wince at my stupidity if I found a way out of the shop, and stumbled into a strange street?

A sudden wave of fatigue swept over me. I was

drained, mentally and physically. I made my way to a rickety swivel chair behind the desk and dropped onto the seat. The decision had been made. My life was in Alexandra Kozhina's hands.

I had almost nodded off in the chair while waiting for Alexandra and Josef to return to the office. When they did, Alexandra exhibited a rare smile, which picked up my spirits.

"Everything is good now," she said.

"It is?" I said, standing.

"Yes. Josef has arranged for us to leave."

"That's good," I said. "I assume we're going back to my hotel, or to the embassy."

"Embassy? *Nyet!!!*" Josef snarled. "No embassy!!!"

I looked to Alexandra, who gave me a shrug of her shoulders, and what I took as a wink. If, as Winston Churchill said, Russia is a riddle wrapped in a mystery inside an enigma, Alexandra Kozhina was its poster girl. She was so mercurial, cool and calculating one moment, playfully girlish the next.

"Are we leaving?" I asked.

"The car will be here soon," Alexandra said.

"To take us where?" I asked.

"To take us to—"

Automobile headlights tossing shards of bright

white light through the shop's front window stopped her in midsentence.

"For us?" I said brightly, seeing in those lights a welcome end to the evening.

"Yes," she said, steel back in her voice, matching the grim expression on her face.

"I'm ready to go," I said.

Alexandra ignored me, turned to Josef, and said, "The back door. Tell Mily we will be at Titanic."

"Now wait a minute," I said. "Who are these people out front?"

"The men who will kill us," Alexandra said.

"But I thought—"

"Mrs. Fletcher, we do not have a moment to spare. You have a choice. Either come with me and spare your life, or stay here and lose it."

Some choice.

Chapter Nineteen

It's been said of me by friends that I can find something positive in even the most unpleasant situations. I experienced one of those moments as we exited Josef's office through a back door, ran down a narrow alley, climbed over a three-foot-high brick wall, and emerged on a street lined with shops and small restaurants.

"Wait," I said, pausing to allow my breath to catch up with me, and to press my hands against pain in my sides.

"Are you all right?" Alexandra asked.

"No, I'm not," I said. "Look, you have to explain to me why we're running away again, and where we're going."

"We're going to Titanic."

"Why? Are we about to sink?"

"No. It is a nightclub. There are people there who will help us."

"A nightclub," I said. "I'll say one thing for you, Ms. Kozhina."

"What is that?"

"At least I'm seeing more of Moscow than my friends are."

She laughed. "I am glad you can see something good in this, Mrs. Fletcher."

Something positive from an unpleasant situation.

A taxi came around the corner, and Alexandra hailed it. Once inside, she told the young driver, "The Titanic, please. And hurry."

I wished she hadn't said that. Russian cab drivers go fast enough without being prompted.

After a fifteen-minute race that brought me close to losing anything I'd eaten that day, we pulled up in front of a building whose flashing neon sign announced TITANIC. A hundred young people milled about outside the entrance, some drinking beer, others openly smoking marijuana cigarettes. Alexandra paid the driver, and we joined the crowd on the sidewalk. Loud music poured through the open front doors. I was aware that I was on the receiving end of some strange looks from the young men and women. Clearly, I was the only person there on the wrong side of forty.

I followed Alexandra past the doors to where two large, scowling men in gray suits stood guard at doors leading to the club itself. The music was now deafening, and we weren't even inside.

"Alexandra, I really don't think that—"

She pulled rubles from her jacket pocket and slapped them on the table. "Dva," she said. I knew from my Russian lessons with Professor Donskoy that it meant two.

One of the men scooped up the money, tore off two tickets from a roll, and handed them to Alexandra. As menacing as he was, at least he was of my generation.

Something positive from an unpleasant situation.

I smiled at him.

He said something in Russian.

"What did he say?" I shouted to Alexandra over the musical din as we were allowed to pass through the interior doors.

"Something dirty. He likes you."

"Oh."

Inside, it was a scene from Fellini, blinding strobe lights casting garish images, the incessant beat of the music assaulting the ears, indeed the whole body, as the booming bass notes pulsated from toes to head. What looked like a thousand young men and women gyrated to the beat on a massive dance floor.

I looked at Alexandra and yelled in her ear, "What do we do now?"

"What?"

"Now. What now?"

She motioned with her head to follow her, and we threaded our way through the twisted, tangled knot of dancers until reaching the opposite end of the dance floor. Men who looked like those at the front door ringed the club's perimeter. Bouncers, I assumed, judging from their size, the hard expression on their faces, and the bulges in their suit jackets. Trouble would not be tolerated in Titanic.

I had the feeling Alexandra wasn't sure of what to do next. Her eyes swept the club, from dancers to bouncers, up to a booth where a disc jockey plied his musical wares, then back to where we stood.

She stepped up onto a round pedestal on which one of the club's many speakers sat, affording her a better overview of her surroundings. I watched her intently; her expression shifted from intense scrutiny, to disbelief, then to overt fear. She hopped down, grabbed my hand, and said, "This way," pulling me toward a door at the corner of the room.

Another back door exit, was all I could think.

Suddenly, we were frozen by the abrupt cessation of the music. I looked to the dance floor, where dancers had frozen, too, players in a game of statues, puzzled expressions creasing their faces.

"Quickly," Alexandra said.

But before we reached the door, a young man intercepted us.

"Mily," Alexandra said.

"Come," the young man said.

We followed him to the opposite corner, where a folding screen concealed yet another door. One of the bouncers, considerably younger than his colleagues, stepped aside as we went behind the screen. Another young man opened the door for us. Alexandra and the two men exchanged words in rapid-fire Russian.

We were in an unlighted hallway. At its end was a heavy metal door, presumably leading to the outside. We were hustled to it, and one of the young men opened it. I was right; we now stood in a small asphalt area between two large Dumpsters. I couldn't see cars, but I could hear their running engines.

We circumvented the Dumpsters to where two Mercedes sedans idled. The young man opened the door to one and shouted something that sounded urgent. Alexandra leaped into the back of the car, turned, and said, "Now, Mrs. Fletcher. Get in!"

Commotion from the hallway reached my ears—shouting, then a gunshot, and anguished Russian words from someone.

I got in the car. The door was slammed closed behind me. The young man who'd led us there ran off, disappearing into the shadows.

The driver turned on the lights and left rubber behind as he made a tight turn and headed for an exit. The second Mercedes followed.

"Where are we going?" I asked.

"To where we will be safe," she said.

"A few days ago I was very safe in my home, in Cabot Cove, Maine."

"And you shall be there again soon. Trust me."

I realized that's exactly what I'd been doing all along. Trusting her. Don't ask me why. Based upon everything that had happened, I shouldn't have trusted anyone. But here I was in another car, being tossed about as the driver made insanely fast turns, on our way to—it almost didn't matter where we were going anymore. I was drained, numb, like someone who'd given up all control and had come to grips with an inevitable future.

As happened earlier that evening on one of my previous mystery rides, we left the city confines and were on country roads. Now, as the countryside flashed by, I began to sense that we were on the same road we'd taken from the airport to Moscow upon arrival in Russia. That both heartened me and was cause for concern.

Why were we heading for the airport?

My instincts proved correct when we turned into

the entrance for Sheremetyevo II International Airport.

"Are we about to fly somewhere?" I asked Alexandra.

"Yes."

"Where?" I envisioned getting on a plane and ending up in Siberia, Mongolia, or worse.

"Home."

"Whose home?"

She turned, grabbed my hand, and said, "Your home, Mrs. Fletcher. And now mine."

Chapter Twenty

As we approached the main terminal, we were joined by other vehicles with flashing lights, which led us to a dark, remote area of the airport. As I strained to see where we were headed, I saw a small twin-engine jet aircraft bathed in white from powerful searchlights mounted atop trucks. We pulled up next to the plane, on the side where a set of stairs extended down.

"We're going on this?" I asked.

Alexandra nodded, opened the door on her side, and got out. I followed.

Armed, uniformed Russian soldiers surrounded the jet. The relief I'd felt a few minutes ago was replaced by renewed fear. The scene was garish—the lights, the low whine of the aircraft's idling engines, the military presence, the uncertainty of it all. I felt like a helpless child, at the mercy of taller, stronger adult strangers.

Alexandra had walked away to speak with a tall, elegant man wearing a suit. I couldn't see his face because of a shadow created by the plane's tail assembly. They stepped out of the shadows and approached me. Now I could see his face. He was undoubtedly American, but I hadn't seen him before. The man smiled and extended his hand. "Harrison Monroe, Mrs. Fletcher. Ready to go?"

"What agency are you with?" I asked, not expecting an answer.

"Plenty of time later to fill you in."

"Where are we going?" I asked.

"A few stops here and there, but then back to the good ol' USA."

"But my clothing and luggage. They're at the hotel."

"They'll be sent. Nothing to worry about. You can pick up something in London."

"London?"

"Yes. Ever been there?"

"Many times, but never under circumstances like this."

Another smile from him. "We'll do everything we can to make the trip comfortable, Mrs. Fletcher. Time to board."

Alexandra looked up into the sky, where millions of stars sparkled against the black scrim, and said,

"Your eyes are like stars in the night," followed by a rueful laugh.

Monroe guided me to the boarding steps with gentle pressure on my elbow, and held my hand from below as I climbed them. As I stepped on board, a man wearing an open-necked white short-sleeved shirt and dark trousers emerged from the cockpit. "Welcome aboard," he said.

"Are you the pilot?" I asked.

"Yes, ma'am."

The aircraft's interior was luxurious. There were two inlaid conference tables with four leather swivel chairs at each, a bar along one wall with gleaming glassware and bottles in wells secured by leather straps, a leather bench seat along the opposite wall, and a lavatory with its door open, revealing the sort of appointments found in the best hotels.

"Please sit here," the pilot said, indicating a chair at one of the tables. "We'll be leaving shortly."

"Am I the only passenger?" I asked.

"Oh, no," he answered. "The others will be here shortly. Soft drink? Something stronger?"

"Tea?"

"It'll take a minute."

"I have a feeling I have nothing but time," I said, folding myself into the luxurious leather that surrounded me and taking a deep breath.

I looked out the small window next to me. The armed soldiers remained in position. The two Mercedes that had brought us here were gone, although the escort vehicles remained, their lights continuing to flash. Alexandra came into view, still talking with the man who'd introduced himself as Harrison Monroe. Although I hadn't met him before, there was a familiarity created by his general appearance and demeanor. It seemed every American government official I'd met since embarking on the trade mission was cut from the same cloth.

They shook hands. A moment later Alexandra was in the plane and seated next to me.

"How do you feel?" she asked.

"Not sure," I said. "Who is he?"

"Mr. Monroe?"

"Yes."

"He works for your government."

"I surmised that. What does he *do* for my government?"

"I am not sure."

"No surprise there," I said.

"Why do you say that?"

"It seems that no one from my government—at least the ones I've dealt with—is comfortable revealing who they work for."

"Ah, Mrs. Fletcher, I can understand your frustration. For me, it is not surprising. In Russia, being secretive is part of our nature. We are born with it. It is in our genes. For you, America is not supposed to have any secrets. When it does, you are shocked."

I looked out the window again and thought about what she'd just said. She was right, I suppose, although I wasn't especially pleased being painted in such a naive light. It really wouldn't have mattered to me how much secrecy my government indulged in if it hadn't involved me.

But it had. As I sat there waiting to take off, I pledged to myself that I would get the answers I wanted, no matter how long it took, or how arduous the process.

The pilot served my tea and asked Alexandra whether she wanted anything.

"Vodka, please," she said. "With ice."

Not only was secrecy an inherent trait of Russians, I thought, so was vodka. Vlady Staritova came to mind. I wished I'd gotten to know him better. Why had he died? Was Karl Warner right, that Vlady hadn't keeled over from natural causes?

Reflection upon Vlady and his death was interrupted by the arrival of a long black limousine, which came to a stop directly beneath my window. It was flanked by two other cars, whose occupants immediately piled out and formed a security gantlet between limo and plane. Obviously, someone of considerable importance had arrived.

I watched as Harrison Monroe went to one of the vehicle's rear doors and spoke to someone inside through a partially open window. He straightened, stepped back, and the door opened.

Vaughan Buckley exited the limo, followed by Olga.

"What's the matter?" Alexandra asked, reacting to my involuntary gasp.

"It's my friends, the Buckleys."

"Good. I was worried about them."

"*You* were worried about them?"

"Yes. We have all been in much danger tonight, Mrs. Fletcher."

I turned to her. "I suggest that after what we've endured together, you call me Jessica."

"I would be honored . . . Jessica."

I had trouble keeping my excitement in check as I waited for Vaughan and Olga to board. They came directly to me, and we embraced. They took the two chairs on the other side of the table and started asking questions.

I held up my hand. "I don't have answers to any of your questions. I wish I did. All I can say is—"

"Who is this?" Vaughan asked, referring to Alexandra.

"Oh," I said, "this is Ms. Alexandra Kozhina."

"The *infamous* Alexandra Kozhina?" Olga asked.

Alexandra smiled demurely. "I am afraid so," she said.

Harrison Monroe boarded, along with two other men I hadn't seen before. One of them joined the pilot in the cockpit and took the right seat. The cockpit door remained open, allowing us to observe the two men manipulate controls, causing the sleek jet to move.

"We're cleared for an immediate takeoff," the copilot said over the intercom. "Please fasten your seat belts and secure any loose objects."

I held my teacup as the pilot applied thrust. The twin engines whined, then roared to life, and we were on our way. In what seemed only a second, the nose tilted up and we were airborne, slicing our way through the night sky to altitude, and destination, unknown.

"Any idea where we're headed?" Vaughan asked.

"They told me London," I replied, "but I wouldn't count on it."

Once we reached cruising altitude, the copilot, who didn't look older than a high school senior, acted as our flight attendant, offering drinks and packaged snacks. I asked who owned the plane.

"It's a beauty, isn't it?" he replied.

Another question deflected.

"You should have something stronger than tea," Vaughan said after he and Olga ordered vodka, and Alexandra asked for her second drink. "After what you've been through."

"Maybe you're right," I said.

While the copilot was busy at the bar, Vaughan leaned over the table and said, "You obviously persuaded Ms. Kozhina to come over to our side."

Alexandra lowered her head, then raised it, looking at me and smiling. "I am sorry to disappoint you, but what you say is not true."

"But you're with us on this plane," Vaughan said.

"That is true," she said. "But—"

Monroe, who sat with his colleague at the other table, suddenly joined us, cutting off what Alexandra was about to say.

"Everyone comfortable?" he asked.

"Ms. Kozhina was about to answer a question," I said.

"Plenty of time for that," Monroe said. "Ms. Kozhina, would you be good enough to join us at the other table? We have some things to discuss with you."

"*Plokha*," I said.

"Pardon?" Monroe said.

"It means bad in Russian, I think," I said. "It's the

worst Russian word I learned. If I'd learned a few more, I'd—"

"Enjoy your drinks," Monroe said. "Pleasure to have you with us."

Chapter Twenty-one

Alexandra's defection to the plane's other table—no pun intended—allowed Vaughan, Olga, and me to catch up on our respective adventures of that night.

"After the men pushed me aside and made you a captive in the limo," Vaughan said, "Olga and I really feared for our lives. They were mobsters, no doubt about that."

"How did you get away from them?" I asked.

Olga answered, "Truth is, Jess, we didn't get away from them. They let us go."

"Immediately?"

"Yes," said Vaughan. "They said something to us in Russian and walked away."

"Just like that?" I said.

"Not quite," Olga said. "One of them spoke some English. He said their expenses had to be paid."

"Expenses? Paid by you? That's outrageous."

Olga laughed. "Sure it was," she said. "A shake-down."

"What did you do?" I asked.

"Paid them, of course," Vaughan said. "Gave them every cent we had in cash. You saw them. Not people to be trifled with."

"You were smart," I said. "At least you're alive. Where did you go after that?"

"We went directly to the embassy," Olga said.

Vaughan chimed in, "We told Mulligan what happened to us, and to you. He didn't seem too concerned. Frankly, I think the man is lacking to be in such a job. A typical bureaucrat waiting for the pension. But enough about us. What happened to you? How did you hook up with her?" He indicated Alexandra, who continued to huddle with Monroe and his colleague.

"It's a—well, I'm not sure I'm capable of telling you with any accuracy. The whole night's a blur."

"You delivered the message to her from Mulligan and Warner, I assume," Olga said.

"Yes, although she already knew what the message was."

"How did she know?"

"How do people know anything in Russia?" I said. "I had the feeling she wasn't interested in working for us. *Us*. I mean the government. The United States.

At any rate, she dismissed it until she received a message on her answering machine. An American male voice said, 'Your eyes are like stars in the night.' "

"Where have I heard that before?" Vaughan asked.

"In the note I carried to her."

"That's right," Vaughan said. "Why would that line change her mind about cooperating with the U.S.?"

"I have no idea," I said. "That's only one of a hundred questions I want answered."

Alexandra rejoined us. "I am sorry," she said. "They had things they wanted me to know. I am also sorry about what happened to all of you. It was not my intention to see you inconvenienced."

My laugh was purely involuntary. "I'm afraid that ranks with one of the great understatements, Alexandra."

"I don't understand," she said.

"It doesn't matter," I said.

I glanced at the other table where Harrison Monroe and his colleague were deep in hushed conversation. Since they didn't seem especially interested in us, it was a good time to ask Alexandra a few questions. I leaned close to her and asked, "What does the message, 'Your eyes are like stars in the night' mean?"

She thought before answering. "It was a way of

letting me know that I was no longer safe with my people.".

"I'll need a little more explanation than that." I said as Vaughan and Olga leaned forward to pick up on our conversation.

"I was told that I would receive instruction from Dimitri on what code word, or words, would be used to alert me to danger."

"Danger? Danger from whom?"

"My Communist comrades."

"Why would you be in danger with them?"

"Because they learned of what I have been doing for your people."

"Wait a minute," Vaughan said, keeping his voice low. "How could your so-called comrades know that you'd decided to cooperate with the Americans? Jess just made the offer tonight. As I understand it from her, you were warned of being in danger before you'd ever decided to cooperate."

A small, satisfied smile crossed her pretty lips. She slowly shook her head, looked at me, then said to Vaughan, "That is not true, Mr. Buckley. I made my decision two years ago."

Chapter Twenty-two

Alexandra's statement that she'd decided two years ago to cooperate with the United States left us stunned. I started to probe her for details, but Monroe again interrupted by ushering her back to his table. It was at that moment that the night caught up with me. I couldn't keep my eyes open, and stopped trying.

When I awoke, Vaughan, too, was sleeping. Olga had moved to the bench seat where she read a fashion magazine, one of many publications available on the plane.

"We're beginning our descent into London," the pilot said over the intercom. "I suggest you tidy up your area in preparation for landing. We should be touching down at Gatwick in about twenty minutes. I'll give you a heads-up when we're a few minutes out."

His announcement woke Vaughan, who yawned, stretched and smiled. "Almost over," he said. "London will be a pleasant change from where we've been."

"And what we've been through," Olga added as she rejoined us.

Flying into London naturally generated thoughts of George Sutherland, Scotland Yard chief inspector and my dear friend. Scottish by birth, George had been with The Yard in London for many years. We'd met there when I was visiting another friend, Majorie Ainsworth, then the world's reigning mystery writer. She was murdered during my visit, which was the catalyst for coming into contact with the dashing, urbane Inspector Sutherland.

We'd maintained our relationship since then, and I'd been a guest at his family's castle in Wick, Scotland, a few summers ago. Some of my close friends back home are convinced George and I were enjoying a romantic relationship. That wasn't true, although I'd be less than honest not to admit that the contemplation was not unpleasant. George had made his feelings known to me during that summer in Wick. But we both knew that if something deeper and more meaningful were ever to develop between us, it could result only from a careful navigation of our individual lives, and what the melding of them would potentially represent. Neither of us had reached that point.

I looked to the other table where Alexandra napped in one of the four chairs. Harrison Monroe and the other man read newspapers.

"Interesting," Vaughan said, "what Ms. Kozhina said about having made up her mind two years ago to change sides. Your delivering that message to her, Jess, seemed to be the catalyst for her to act on her decision."

"I suppose so," I said. "Still, why would she wait so long?"

Monroe joined us. "We'll be landing in a few minutes," he said. "I'm sure you'll be happy to get into a comfortable hotel and catch up on your sleep."

"I have other things on my mind besides sleep," I said.

"Oh? A writer's mind at work?"

"Nothing to do with being a writer," I said. "More a matter of being a citizen of the United States."

"Meaning?"

"Meaning, Mr. Monroe, that what we've been put through since agreeing to be part of a trade mission hardly represents what any citizen should be subjected to. No one responds to questions. We're told to do things without any explanation, any justification. Here we are on a private jet flying to London after being spirited out of Moscow. Our personal belongings are left behind. My friends here are accosted by Russian hoodlums. I was kidnapped, chased through the streets, hustled from car to car, and taken on mad rides in and out of Moscow, all because I was, as they say, a good soldier, doing what I was asked to do by my government."

Monroe listened quietly, his chin resting on a tent formed by his hands.

Vaughan said, "I think what Mrs. Fletcher is saying, Mr. Monroe, is that some simple answers would go a long way to salving the resentment she's feeling—that we're all feeling."

"That shouldn't be a problem," Monroe said.

"Exactly," I said. "It shouldn't be a problem. But it seems to be a big one."

"Ladies and gentlemen, we're about six minutes from touchdown," the pilot announced. "Please take your seats and buckle up, secure any loose items."

Monroe stood. "There's a meeting scheduled first thing in the morning," he said. "I'm sure you'll have all the answers you need. Excuse me."

The landing was so smooth we barely felt the wheels touch the runway. As the pilot taxied to a hangar on the perimeter of the airport, I saw through the window two limousines with their headlights on, and what appeared to be a police vehicle. A number of people milled about as the plane was maneuvered to position the boarding stairs close to the vehicles.

The pilot stepped into the passenger compartment, but Monroe held up a hand. "We just need a few minutes," he said. The pilot quickly retreated into the cockpit, shutting the door behind him.

Monroe addressed us: "I understand the frustration you've felt the past few days. All I can say at this juncture is that everything was done with your best interests uppermost in mind. Tomorrow morning you'll be meeting with the people who are authorized to explain what has happened, and to answer your questions. Until that meeting, I ask that you put aside any preconceived notions, not discuss the matter with anyone except among yourselves, enjoy a good dinner and the rest of the evening, and be ready to go to tomorrow's meeting at nine sharp."

"What about clothing?" Olga asked. "And toiletries."

"Our London people were contacted before we left Moscow. We gave them our best estimate of what you would need until your belongings arrive tomorrow afternoon. You have sleepwear, toiletries, and fresh undergarments and other items of clothing in your hotel rooms. If we were off on our estimate of your sizes, I apologize. Any other questions?"

"Where are we staying?" Vaughan asked.

"One of London's finest," Monroe replied. "Nothing too good for citizens like you."

Monroe knocked on the cockpit door, and the pilot emerged. "Ready to go," Monroe said.

The passenger door opened, and the boarding stairs were lowered. Monroe and his colleague kept Alexandra behind with them as Vaughan, Olga, and I descended the stairs to the tarmac, where we were greeted by a young woman in a tailored brown business suit. She was flanked by a half-dozen men.

"This way, please," she said in a clipped British accent, and led us to one of the limos.

I looked back to see Alexandra come down the boarding stairs, Monroe in front of her, the other man taking up the rear. They were ushered into the second limousine.

"Why wouldn't he at least tell us where we're staying?" Olga asked.

Vaughan answered, "Because it's the government, my dear."

"But it's *our* government."

"Precisely."

Gatwick, the second of the two major London airports, is thirty miles south of the city, approximately twice as far as the more frequently used Heathrow. It took us about an hour to reach our hotel, which I recognized immediately—the Athenaeum, on Picca-dilly, one of my favorite London hotels.

But instead of pulling up to its entrance, the driver stopped a half block away, in front of a row of stately town houses belonging to the Athenaeum. I'd been given a tour of one of them during my last stay; they define elegance and privacy. Guests staying in them have their own entrance, yet enjoy the full array of services offered by the hotel itself.

The two limousines had been followed into the city by three other cars. Now, with all five vehicles lined up at the curb, we got out and were immediately led up the stairs of the town houses. I stood on the small landing and looked to where Vaughan and Olga were entering the house next to me. On my other side, Alexandra Kozhina and the British woman who'd greeted us at the foot of the aircraft stairs were about to go into that building.

I was personally escorted into my quarters by Har-rison Monroe. Once we were inside, he said, "I trust you'll find this comfortable enough, Mrs. Fletcher."

"Of course," I said.

There was a knock at the door. Monroe opened it, and a young woman, of the same stripe as the one with Alexandra, entered.

"Mrs. Fletcher, this is Ms. Connie McGlouthern.

She works closely with us and will be staying with you in the second bedroom."

I suppose my expression of surprise was evident, because he added, "Hope you don't mind the company. Necessary, but only for tonight. Tomorrow, you'll be on your way home to—where is it you live?—Cabot Cove? In Maine?"

"No, I don't mind," I said. "And going home to Cabot Cove sounds lovely."

"I'm sure it does. Well, I'll leave you two until we meet up again at dinner. An hour. Connie will bring you."

"Are we eating in the hotel?" I asked.

"Yes. A room reserved for us. See you then."

After a few words of greeting Ms. McGlouthern showed me where a variety of clothing and toiletries had been placed in the master bedroom. "I'll leave you alone until dinner, Mrs. Fletcher," she said, her brogue pegging her Scottish heritage.

I thought of George Sutherland.

"That will be fine," I said. "I have a personal call to make to someone here in London."

"I'm afraid that won't be possible," she said.

"Why not?"

"Orders are that you and the others are not to make any calls until after the meeting tomorrow morning."

"That's outrageous," I said. "How dare anyone tell me I can't call a friend?"

"Please, Mrs. Fletcher, perhaps Mr. Monroe will explain at dinner. But I have my orders. The phones in the town houses have been disconnected for tonight."

She saw how upset I was, and wisely left the bedroom. I sat on the king-size bed and fought to bring my anger under control. Once I had, I went to a window that looked out over Piccadilly and saw two of the men who'd been at Gatwick when we deplaned. Obviously, not only weren't we allowed to make calls, we wouldn't be going out for a midnight stroll, either.

An hour later, Ms. McGlouthern and I exited the town house, walked a few yards down the street, entered the hotel, and stepped into a small private dining room, where Monroe, his unnamed colleague, Vaughan and Olga, Alexandra Kozhina and two other men were seated at an elaborately set table. The men stood. "Good evening again, Mrs. Fletcher," Monroe said. He pointed to the only unoccupied chair. "Please. Next to me."

Everyone looked appropriately exhausted; conversation at the dinner table was mundane and without spirit. There was a natural temptation to fling questions at Monroe and the other men, all of whom had been introduced by name, but with no more identification than that. It wasn't worth pursuing what agencies they represented. The answers would undoubtedly be as they'd been all along—nonanswers, evasions, vague references, outright ignoring of any such inquiries.

Dinner was simple, and quickly served; we were there no longer than an hour. Afterward, we were reminded that we'd be picked up at nine o'clock for the meeting—breakfast would be served at it—and were told we were booked the following night, first class, on British Airways, for New York's Kennedy Airport. The afternoon was ours to enjoy at our leisure. Our luggage would arrive from Moscow prior to leaving London.

My final thought before falling asleep was that tomorrow was Sunday. I'd lost all sense of time.

I slept fitfully, which was to be expected, but was ready to go by eight-thirty. The limos took us from the Athenaeum to the American Embassy on Grosvenor Square, a bunker of a building I'd visited a few times during previous London trips.

The gigantic bald eagle atop the building peered down at us as we entered, and were immediately taken to a conference room on the ground floor. After partaking in a breakfast buffet and coffee/tea service set up in a corner of the large room, we took seats and waited for the meeting to begin.

We didn't have to wait long. The door opened, and Harrison Monroe entered, followed by another tall, slim gentleman wearing a form-fitting double-breasted blue blazer, crisp white shirt, red-and-white tie, and gray slacks. His silver hair was carefully coifed, and he carried himself with the carriage of someone at home in all situations, and with any group of people.

"Good morning," he said. "I'm John Vogler, attached to the embassy's commerce office. I understand you've had quite an experience in Moscow." His smile was slight, practiced.

"I understand we're here to receive some answers to questions," I said.

"To the extent I'm able to answer them, yes."

His qualification nettled me.

"Let me begin by giving you some information that will probably answer some of those questions. As you know, Ms. Kozhina has been an important member of a group within Russia dedicated to overthrowing the duly elected democratic government of Boris Yeltsin."

We looked at Alexandra, who did not seem especially comfortable on center stage.

Vogler continued. "Because she's been so intimately involved with the leaders of that movement, her knowledge of its inner workings have not only been of great interest to President Yeltsin's government, it has important ramifications for the United States.''

He now looked at me.

''It is not easy for me to admit to a failure by individuals who work for our government, but I'm afraid that is exactly what I must do this morning.''

''Failure?'' Vaughan said. ''What sort of failure?''

''Without being specific, I—''

''We'd appreciate it if you would *be* specific, Mr. Vogler,'' I said. ''We've been subjected to enough bureaucratic vagueness to last a lifetime.''

If I was too forthright and candid, he didn't reflect it. He smiled at me, nodded, and went on with his speech.

''I'm sure you are aware that due to national security considerations, complete candor is not always possible. But I'll be as frank as permissible. Our relationship with Ms. Kozhina goes back two years. It started when—''

''Excuse me for interrupting,'' I said, ''but what you've just said astounds me. I carried a message to Alexandra—Ms. Kozhina—on behalf of people within my own government. I was told by those people that it was important to convince her to come over to our side, I suppose it's called, to act as a . . . double agent? . . . I'm not familiar with the nomenclature of the spy business. She decided to do that last night."

Vogler started to say something, but Alexandra interrupted. "No, Jessica, I did not decide to do that last night. I decided to do that two years ago, and have been doing it ever since."

"But then why send me?" I asked, unable to control sounding strident.

"That was the failure I mentioned earlier," said Vogler. "The U.S. government is, as you well know, very large. There are times that duplication of effort occurs, an overlapping of function, generally well-meaning, but problematic."

I turned to Alexandra, who looked away.

I said, "What you're telling me, Mr. Vogler, is that what I went through was unnecessary, a mistake, a 'duplication of effort,' as you put it."

"Yes, Mrs. Fletcher. That's correct."

"And Ms. Kozhina has been working as a double agent for two years?"

"Correct again."

"The people who asked me to deliver the message had no idea that she'd already been recruited? *Two years ago?*"

"Sad, but true. Two different agencies at work, one not knowing what the other was doing."

Vaughan's voice was louder as he asked, "What two agencies?"

Vogler grimaced. "I'm afraid I'm not at liberty to reveal that, Mr. Buckley. Suffice it to say, they both function in the intelligence community."

Vaughan sat back and let out a series of unintelligible utterances that were best left that way.

"I understand your dismay," said Vogler, "but these are the facts."

I turned to Alexandra. "If you'd been functioning as a double agent for two years," I said, "why did you encourage me to meet with you?"

"For two reasons," she said. "First, I wished to meet you. You are a writer I look up to very much. It was an honor—I was excited to meet such a famous writer."

"That's flattering, Alexandra, but considering what it led to, I can't view it with much enthusiasm."

"I can understand that," she said.

"You said there were two reasons. What's the second?"

She looked at Vogler, whose raised eyebrows said he was waiting for the answer, too.

"It is all right to say?" she asked him.

He nodded.

"Things were becoming tense," she said softly, eyes trained on the tabletop. "We knew that my situation was becoming serious, even dangerous. Too many people had learned that I was not loyal to the cause. Two years is a long time to lead a double life, Jessica."

"But what did that have to do with me?"

"The note from—" Another look for approval from Vogler.

"Go ahead," he said.

"The note from Dimitri," she said. "It was important I receive it."

"Why?" Vaughan asked.

"Because it contained the code phrase to be used in case it was necessary for me to leave immediately."

"Your eyes are like stars in the night," I said.

"Yes. That was the phrase. It was placed in a certain part of the note. The fifth sentence. I knew that if I heard that, it was time to get out."

I started to respond, but Vaughan cut me off. "Let me see if I have this sorted out," he said. "You have two intelligence agencies working at cross purposes where Ms. Kozhina is concerned. One recruited her two years ago, and she's been functioning for that agency ever since. The other agency wants to recruit Ms. Kozhina, too, only it doesn't know that the goal has already been accomplished.

"Jessica—Mrs. Fletcher—is given a note to be delivered to Ms. Kozhina in Moscow. In that note is a coded phrase. The other intelligence agency, the one operating in the dark, if you will, finds out that Mrs. Fletcher has the note, and will make contact with Ms. Kozhina. They, whoever they are, see this as an opportunity to recruit Ms. Kozhina, and ask Mrs. Fletcher to attempt to accomplish that. Correct so far?"

"You're doing very well," Vogler said. "Proceed."

"Anything you want to add, Jess?" Vaughan asked.

"Not at the moment," I said, pleased with the clarity of his summary.

"Actually," Vaughan said, "that pretty much is what I've figured out so far."

"Let me ask a question," Olga said. She'd been silent since the meeting began. "Why were we forcibly separated from Mrs. Fletcher by men who clearly were mobsters? Mafioso, Russian style."

"To protect you," Alexandra said.

"Protect us?" Olga blurted. "We were physically shoved aside, then shaken down for money. You call that being protected?"

"It was better that only Jessica visit me," Alexandra said. "As for the men wanting money, that is the

273

way they are. The Communist cause and the mafia have similar goals. Unfortunate, but true."

"Were you in physical danger?" Olga asked me.

"I think so," I replied. "It certainly seemed that way."

"We were both in danger," Alexandra said. "But only because—" She stopped speaking and again looked at Vogler. "I do not wish to offend," she said.

"Feel free," said Vogler.

"It was having Mrs. Fletcher come to me with a request that I change my allegiance that placed us in physical danger."

I started to respond, but she cut me off. "You see, Jessica, those within my movement who suspected me of not being loyal—and that's all it was, suspicion—decided, I think, that you would be persuasive enough to convince me. Fortunately, I received a warning on my answering machine, which gave us time to escape."

"By the skin of our teeth," I said. "They were never far behind."

A brief discussion ensued about plans for leaving London that night. As it went on, my thoughts went to Vlady Staritova and Ward Wenington. I waited until there was a lull in the conversation before saying, "Two men have died since I came on this so-called trade mission, Mr. Vogler. One worked for our government, a gentleman named Ward Wenington. I discovered his body in Washington. Then, at a dinner in Moscow, my Russian publisher, Vladislav Staritova, dropped dead. I was told that neither death resulted from natural causes. Perhaps you'd be good enough to bring me up to date."

"Sorry, Mrs. Fletcher, but I don't have any information about those deaths."

We locked eyes. I didn't believe him, and he knew it.

Vogler went on to discuss other matters, none of which were substantive. Twenty minutes later, the meeting ended.

"Your flight leaves tonight at nine, from Heathrow," Vogler said. "Between now and then, you are free to enjoy this great city. Your luggage from Moscow will be delivered to your rooms at the Athenaeum by two this afternoon. Transportation to the airport will leave the hotel at seven. Any questions?"

"I have one," I said.

"Yes, Mrs. Fletcher?"

"I was prohibited last night from placing any phone calls. I'd like an explanation of why that freedom was denied me, and the others."

Vogler shrugged and said, "A practical necessity, Mrs. Fletcher. It's no longer necessary to restrict you. Feel free to call anyone you wish."

As we filed from the room, Vaughan said, "There's a book in this."

"If you feel that way," Vogler said, "you'll follow through and publish it. We're all beneficiaries of our Constitution's First Amendment, a precious right never to be violated. Thank you for being here this morning, and for the contribution you've made to your country."

We stood on the street and looked at each other. The limousines were gone. So were the men who'd escorted us. We were alone with each other, and on our own.

"Slick fellow," Vaughan said.

"Too slick," Olga said. "Who do you think he works for?"

"The CIA, Defense Intelligence Agency, some other spook agency," Vaughan said. "There are dozens of them."

Alexandra hadn't left the building with us, and we assumed that because of her status and situation, she'd be kept in some sort of seclusion.

But to our surprise, she joined us.

"I meant what I said in there, Ms. Kozhina," Vaughan said, "about there being a book. Obviously, you have quite a story to tell."

"I don't think I could ever do that," she said.

Vaughan handed her his card. "If you ever want

to explore it, Ms. Kozhina, give me a call. That's my private number."

"I'm surprised to see you," I said to her. "We assumed you'd be sequestered somewhere."

She laughed. "I thought I would be, too. No, they told me I'm free to do anything I want."

"You are coming on the plane with us tonight?"

"Oh, no. I am staying here in London for a few days, perhaps a week."

"What are you doing this afternoon?" I asked.

"I don't know."

"What about you, Jess?" Olga asked.

"I thought I'd call my friend George Sutherland and see if he's in town and free for lunch."

The smile on Vaughan and Olga's faces said many things. I ignored their editorial content.

"Would you be free for lunch?" I asked Alexandra.

"Yes."

"Then we'll have lunch together, whether George can make it or not. Vaughan? Olga?"

"Thanks, no," Vaughan said. "As long as we've ended up in London, there are some things we'd like to do before leaving tonight."

"Suit yourself," I said.

We said good-bye; we'd see each other again at the hotel.

I called George's office number from a red public

phone booth. To my delight he was there, surprised to hear from me and free for lunch. When I told him we'd be joined by a newfound Russian friend, he said he looked forward to meeting her, and suggested we rendezvous at noon at Brasserie on the Park, in the Park Lane Hotel on Piccadilly, near Hyde Park Corner.

"I just thought of something," I told Alexandra after hanging up.

"What is that?"

"Since today is Sunday, you might want to see democracy in action—*really* in action."

"Oh?"

"Hyde Park Corner is always very busy on Sunday mornings. It's where anyone can get up and speak their piece, preach, rant and rave, and sometimes even have something worthwhile to say. It's very exciting. I think you'll enjoy it. Besides, we're having lunch close to there. Game?"

"Pardon?"

"Game. Would you like to?"

"Very much, yes. I am happy to go wherever you go, Jessica."

Chapter Twenty-three

We made our way into the maze of underground tunnels that allowed pedestrians to safely cross the busy streets surrounding the park. The events of the past few days were now very much behind me, although the unexplained deaths of Vladislav Staritova and Ward Wenington kept invading my consciousness.

Still, I felt buoyant. I liked being with Alexandra Kozhina. She was a bright, interesting young woman whose Russian roots were a source of fascination to me. We chatted like schoolgirl chums on our way to the park, laughing at some of the things we'd shared in the past forty-eight hours. Of course, my feeling of well-being was also bolstered by the promise of seeing George Sutherland at lunch.

The park was especially busy that morning. Speakers had staked out territory, and were in the midst of their appeals to the curious who'd gathered that Sunday morning to experience one of the world's great free markets of thought and ideas.

Some speakers simply yelled loud enough to gather a crowd. Others peddled their intellectual wares from atop boxes, and used portable sound systems and elaborate visual aids to be better understood. Their causes ranged from animal rights—No nation in the world loves its pets more than England—to off-beat religious theories. East Indians called for the abolition of their government, while a Chinese speaker condemned the handing off of Hong Kong to Communist rule. A disheveled older man with matted hair down his back and over his face, warned, at the top of his lungs, that sinners had thirty-six hours to repent before doomsday. And a woman wearing a witch's costume, replete with broad-brimmed spiked hat and holding a broom, claimed that witchcraft had infiltrated the British Parliament, and was behind its decisions.

"Enjoying yourself?" I asked Alexandra as we moved from speaker to speaker.

"Very much. Such fun. There is more free speech now in Russia, but not like this."

The area devoted to this Sunday morning spectacle is large, which was why, I suppose, I noticed a particular gentleman who seemed always to be where we were. He was well dressed, wearing a tan raincoat and plaid cap, highly polished brown shoes, and carrying a rolled-up black umbrella. The umbrella struck me as odd, considering the splendid sunny day. But the British are fond of carrying things no matter what the weather, including walking sticks and their beloved "brollies."

We stopped at an ice-cream vendor and bought two cones—vanilla for me, chocolate for Alexandra.

"I've been meaning to ask you," I said, "about the message on your answering machine. 'Your eyes are like stars in the night.' Who left that message?"

"My handler."

"Handler?"

"A term, that's all. Mr. Warner left it."

"Karl Warner. He was your 'handler?' "

"Yes. After Mr. Wenington died."

"You knew about that?"

"Oh, yes."

"Do you know how Wenington died?"

"No," she said, taking a lick of her ice cream.

"Was he murdered?"

"I don't know. This is good ice cream. Better than in Moscow."

"I'm sure the ice cream will improve there, too," I said, "along with many other things."

We continued to stroll, eventually stopping where

a young man and woman spoke into a microphone of their fervent belief that socialism was the only answer to world famine and disease. I observed Alexandra's reaction to what they said. She winced at some of their claims, seemed passively in agreement with others.

As we listened, I took in the eclectic mix of men, women, and children, old and young, prosperous and downtrodden, who surrounded us. The same man who ended up at every stop we made was there again, listening intently. He'd moved to Alexandra's side, not looking at her, his attention focused on the orators.

I was about to return my focus to them, too. But just before I did, I saw him move his umbrella in such a way to point its tip at Alexandra's ankle.

I looked up at the stage. A moment later, Alexandra yelped, crouched, and scratched her ankle.

The man was gone.

"You all right?" I asked.

"Yes," she said, straightening. "Must have been bitten by something."

"That man," I said, pointing to his back as he disappeared into the throng of people.

"What man?"

"Him."

"Who?"

"Nothing. Ready to leave?"

"Yes."

We started in the direction of the tunnels leading beneath the roads, and had gotten a few hundred yards when Alexandra grabbed my arm.

"Are you feeling ill?" I asked.

"Yes. I—"

She collapsed in my arms as though someone had pulled a plug, draining her of every fiber.

I lowered her to the grass and looked into her face. Her eyes had rolled back, leaving only the whites visible. Her pretty face was bathed in sweat, and her whole body had begun to shake.

I looked up at people who'd stopped to observe.

"Help, please," I said. "Get an ambulance. She's . . . she's dying!"

Chapter Twenty-four

An onlooker dialed 911 from a cell phone, and minutes later an ambulance and two police officers arrived. Alexandra was placed on a stretcher and gently moved into the rear of the ambulance.

"Are you with her?" one of two medical emergency workers asked me.

"Yes."

"Come on then."

I sat on a small jump seat next to Alexandra while the technician administered an IV. "Casualty department's been alerted," he said, not looking up from his task.

"Casualty department?"

"Yank, huh? Emergency room, you'd call it."

"Oh."

"Any notion what happened to her?" he asked.

"No. She—I saw a man with an umbrella. He touched her leg with its tip."

"Man with a brolly?" The technician stopped asking any more questions of me.

Traffic was wicked, but we eventually reached Charing Cross Hospital, where nurses and doctors anxiously awaited our arrival. I followed as Alexandra was wheeled inside and through swinging doors into the casualty department. A young physician in a white coat approached. "A word, ma'am?"

"Of course."

He asked me a series of questions, few of which I could answer. It was especially difficult when he got into who she was, family background, and other personal questions that put me on the spot. Do I explain why she was in London and suggest they call the American Embassy? I decided to stop worrying about it and be as honest as possible.

"Russian, you say," the doctor said. "A bit of a spy?"

"I wouldn't say that," I said. "The embassy people are better equipped to explain."

I told him about the man in raincoat and cap who'd touched the tip of his umbrella to Alexandra's ankle, deliberately as far as I was concerned. He listened with apparent interest, making notes as I spoke. When I was finished, he looked up at me, nodded, and said, "Can't see what that would have to do with her sudden illness, but I'll mention it to the attending physicians."

"Any idea how she's doing?" I asked.

"I'll check, be back in a bit. Make yourself comfortable in the waiting room."

"Is there a phone I can use?" I asked.

"Use this one here, Mrs. . . ."

"Fletcher. Jessica Fletcher."

"The mystery writer?"

"Yes."

• "Seems we've got a bit of a mystery here ourselves."

George Sutherland answered at Scotland Yard headquarters. I told him what had happened, and where I was.

"I'm on my way," he said.

We had tea in the hospital cafeteria.

"Wonderful to see you, Jess," George said.

"Same here, although a pleasant lunch would have been preferable."

"Tell me about this young woman."

I spent the next ten minutes doing just that. When I'd completed my tale, he sat back in his chair, shook his head, and said, "Trouble follows you like that character in your American comic strip, the one with the rain cloud always over his head."

"If I thought that," I said, "I'd never venture out of the house again."

"Might not be a bad idea. Tell me more about this bloke with the umbrella."

I did.

"Interesting," he said.

"I thought so."

"Had a case a number of years ago, Jess. Height of the cold war, bloody damn spies running about killing other spies to God knows what end. At any rate, one of these shadowy types was poisoned."

"And?"

"Seems it was administered by a rigged brolly, spring-action device at its tip, shoot the poison into the victim who doesn't even know it happened until—"

"Until he died," I said, grimly.

"That's right."

"Do you think that's what might have happened to Alexandra?"

"No idea, but it's worth mentioning to the doctors, wouldn't you say?"

"Absolutely."

"Come on, then, let's find one."

It was a two-way exchange of information. The doctor listened closely to George, obviously impressed with his credentials and knowledge. "Could be ricin," George said. "A bloody toxic substance, for certain. As bad as botulinus. Fashioned from castor oil beans. Bloody difficult to detect—unless you're looking for it."

The doctor said, "I doubt if we have the capability to detect it, Inspector."

"Wouldn't expect that you would," George said. "But our lab chaps at The Yard have dealt with it before. I suggest you confer with them. Here's the direct number."

"I'll call right away," the doctor said.

"How is she?" I asked him before he left.

His face reflected the gravity of the situation. "Alive," he said, "but barely. The next twenty-four hours will tell the tale."

As we left the hospital, I felt as though a thousand-pound weight had been placed on my shoulders.

"She won't make it, will she?" I said as we walked away from the hospital with no particular destination.

"If it's ricin, I would say the chances are very slim, Jess. But maybe it was another substance, a less lethal one."

"Let's hope for that."

"Still want to have lunch?"

"Yes. I'm leaving London tonight. I'd like as much time with you as possible."

Over onion soup and salads at the Brasserie on the

Park, we tried to cram into the few hours we had as much conversation as possible. I expressed my admiration for Alexandra Kozhina, and wondered whether I should postpone leaving London.

"I think under the circumstances, Jess, you'd best get on that plane tonight. No sense upsetting the powers that be. I'll keep close tabs on your Russian friend, and be in touch with you on a regular basis."

"I suppose I should call the embassy. They'll be looking for her."

"Yes, I suppose you should." He frowned, looked me in the eye, and said, "Your Russian adventure might not be over, you know. This business of the chap ending up dead in Washington, and your Russian publisher keeling over, leaves a sizable cloud over things."

"Not as far as I'm concerned," I said.

"I hope that's true, Jess. But you discovered the body in Washington, and were with your publisher when he died. If the scenario is true—that Ms. Kozhina was the target of an assassination—you were there, too, when it happened."

"If I think about that, George, I'll spend the rest of my life looking over my shoulder. I won't live that way."

I spoke again with George that night from Heathrow Airport, moments before I boarded the

British Airways' 747 for the flight to New York. The news was heartening. Scotland Yard's forensic scientists had worked with the hospital in determining what had happened to Alexandra. It wasn't ricin, thank God, but a less lethal form of poison, and a known antidote was being administered. Although she was still in critical condition, the physicians felt there was a good chance she'd pull through. Without George and his experts, I know she would have died.

I stayed in New York overnight at Vaughan and Olga's apartment in the Dakota, and flew to Maine the following morning. It was good to be home, although I didn't experience the sort of pleasure I usually do when returning from a trip. My friends called and wanted to get together for a welcome-home party, but I declined as politely as possible, saying that the trip had been arduous, and that I was suffering a terminal case of jet lag.

George called every night with a progress report on Alexandra. Poor girl. Although she'd survived the attack, the poison had compromised some of her internal organs. She was in for months of convalescence in a London nursing home arranged for her by unnamed officials of the American and British governments.

I obtained the nursing home address and dropped frequent notes to her, which she promptly answered.

She was feeling stronger each day, she said, and looked forward to a full recovery.

Two months later, while enjoying breakfast on my patio, I received a call from Vaughan Buckley. "Sitting down?" he asked.

"No, but there's a chair nearby."

"Jess, Alexandra Kozhina is in New York. I just got off the phone with her."

"That's wonderful," I said. "How long is she staying?"

"Just overnight. She heads for Washington in the morning. Olga and I are having dinner with her. I think she's interested in writing the book I suggested."

"Interesting."

"I was wondering whether you could get down here to join us. I know it's extremely short notice, but I figured it might be possible. Still friends with that fellow who runs his own airline in Cabot Cove?"

"Jed Richardson? Sure. But he's away on a charter, left this morning."

"Shame. No way you could make it?"

"You know I'd love to, Vaughan, but I just don't see it happening. But you will give her my love."

"Of course. Maybe she'll have a chance to call you before she leaves."

I no sooner hung up when the phone rang again. It was Alexandra.

"I just spoke with Vaughan," I said. "He told me about dinner, and that you might write that book."

"I'm thinking of it," she said. "I wish I could see you, Jessica. I feel very much as though we're sisters or something, close friends."

"I feel the same way, Alexandra. We went through a lot together."

She laughed. "That, as you would say, is a large understatement. I'll be going directly back to London from Washington."

"What are you doing there?" I asked.

She hesitated before saying, "Oh, just meeting with a few people."

Translation: I can't talk about it.

We chatted for a few more minutes, promised to one day meet again, and the conversation ended. I suffered parallel joy and sadness at having spoken with her. She obviously was still immersed in some sort of clandestine activity of the sort that, based upon my brush with it, was something I would assiduously avoid for the rest of my life.

Alexandra Kozhina did write her book for Buckley House. Vaughan told me he was extremely pleased with the manuscript she delivered. I asked questions about it, but he was evasive, saying only, "She wants to send you one of the first copies, Jess, autographed to you."

"I look forward to that. Please give her my love when you see her again."

A year later, a FedEx package arrived from Buckley House. I eagerly opened it to find a copy of Alexandra's book, *A Sub-Rosa Life*.

I opened it to the dedication page:

> *FOR: Jessica Fletcher, an inspiration to any aspiring writer, a courageous woman, and one of the most decent human beings I have ever known. With love. Alexandra.*

Vaughan called that afternoon.

"Get that book?" he asked.

"Yes. I was very touched. I cried."

"It's a fine work, Jess, well-written and illuminating."

"I look forward to reading it."

"I'll be anxious for your reaction. Naturally, there is some material that couldn't be included."

"Sensitive material?"

"Yes. You should know that Vlady Staritova was murdered, the same poison used on Alexandra."

"How do you know that?"

"From Alexandra. He'd learned about her double

life, and pursued her to write a book for him about it, pursued too aggressively, I'm afraid."

"Who killed him?" I asked.

"Alexandra's not sure. Could have been her own people trying to shut him up. Or, it might have involved the other side."

" 'The other side?' *Our* side?"

"She doesn't know."

It was summer, but I felt a pervasive chill that caused me to shudder.

"Wenington, too?" I asked.

"We'll never know that, Jess. Those are the sort of questions that never get answered because the people involved don't want them answered. At any rate, enjoy the book."

"Where is Alexandra?" I asked.

"I don't know the answer to that, either. We hoped to send her on a promotion tour, but we can't find her."

"Can't find her?"

"Yup. Nothing reaches her in London, no forwarding address."

"The embassy? Have you tried them?"

"Sure. They say they have no idea where she's gone. Actually, it will probably help sell the book. Author was a spy, writes about it, then disappears into the night."

"I suppose so," I said. "Well, thanks, Vaughan. I'll treasure the book, and her kind words to me in it."

"Take care. Be in touch soon."

I never heard from Alexandra Kozhina again. Each time I thought of her, I became weepy, and so I tried to stop thinking about her, with some success.

But there are times, usually odd moments, and for odd reasons, that her face flashes before me, and I wonder where she is and what she's doing.

I'm sure I'll never know.

Read on for a preview of
Murder, She Wrote:
A Little Yuletide Murder
available from Signet.

"The meeting will come to order!"

We'd gathered in the Cabot Cove Memorial Hall, built after World War II to honor those from our town who'd given their lives, literally and figuratively, defending the country. It soon became a popular place for meetings and social events, especially when large numbers of people were involved. This meeting to plan the upcoming annual Christmas festival certainly qualified. The hall was packed with citizens, most of whom came simply to listen—or to get out of the house during that dreary first week of December—and for some to offer their ideas on what this year's festival should involve.

I was delighted to be there, not only because I enjoyed participating in the planning, but because for the first time in years, I would actually be home during the holiday season. I'd found myself traveling on too many previous holidays, usually to promote my newest murder mystery, or sometimes simply because invitations extended to me were too appealing to pass up. But even though I'd spent previous Christmases in some wonderful, even exotic locations, I always felt a certain ache and emptiness at being away from my dear friends, and from the town I called home and loved, Cabot Cove, Maine.

The meeting was chaired by our mayor, Jim Shevlin. Seated with him at a long table on a raised platform were representatives from the public library, the Chamber of Commerce, the town historical society (sometimes snidely known as the "town hysterical society"), local political clubs, the fire and police departments, the volunteer ambulance corps, and local hospital, schools, and, of course, the standing decorating committee, who, each year, turned our lovely small village into a festival of holiday lights.

Shevlin again called for order, and people eventually took seats and ended their conversations.

"It's gratifying to see so many of you here this morning," Shevlin said, an engaging smile breaking across his face. "This promises to be the biggest and best holiday festival ever."

People applauded, including me and Dr. Seth Hazlitt, my good friend with whom I sat in the front row. He leaned close to my ear and said, "Jimmy always says it's going to be the biggest and the best."

I raised my eyebrows, looked at Seth, and said, "And it usually is."

"Hard for you to say, Jessica," Seth said, "considerin' you haven't been here in a spell."

"But from what I hear, each year tops the previous one. Besides, I'll be here this year."

"And a good thing you will," Seth said. "This is where Jessica Fletcher ought to be spendin' her Christmases."

I was used to mild admonishment from Seth, knowing he always meant well, even though his tone could be taken at times as harsh and scolding. I returned my attention to the dais, where Shevlin introduced the chairwoman of the decorating committee.

She went through a long list of things the committee planned to do this year, including renting for the first time a large searchlight that would project a red-and-green light into the sky above the town. This resulted in a heated debate about whether it was too commercial and tacky for Cabot Cove. Eventually, Mayor Shevlin suggested the searchlight idea be put on hold until further discussions could be held.

As such meetings tend to do, this one dragged on beyond a reasonable length. It seemed everyone wanted to have a say, and did. It was during the presentation of how Cabot Cove's schoolchildren would participate that I noticed someone missing from the dais. I turned to Seth. "Where's Rory?" I asked.

Seth leaned forward and scanned the faces at the long table. "You're right, Jessica," he said. "Rory hasn't missed a holiday planning meeting for as long as I can remember."

Rory Brent was a prosperous local farmer who'd played Santa Claus at our holiday festival for the past fifteen years. He was born to the role. Brent was a big, outgoing man with a ready, infectious laugh. He easily weighed two hundred and fifty pounds, and had a full head of flowing white hair and a bushy white beard to match. No makeup needed: He *was* Santa Claus. His custom was to attend the planning meeting fully dressed in his Santa costume. He proudly dragged it out of mothballs each year, stitched up gaps in the seams, and had it cleaned and pressed before the meeting.

"Is he ill?" I asked.

"Saw him yesterday," Seth said. "Down at Charlene's Bakery. Looked healthy enough to me."

"He must have been detained. Maybe some emergency at the farm."

"Ayuh," Seth muttered.

A few minutes later, when Jim Shevlin invited further comments from the audience, Seth stood and asked why Rory Brent wasn't there.

"I had Margaret try to call him at the farm," Shevlin said. Margaret was deputy mayor of Cabot Cove. He looked to where she sat at his right.

She reported into her microphone, "I called a few times but there's no answer."

"Maybe somebody ought to take a ride out to the farm," Seth suggested from the floor.

"Good idea," said Shevlin. "Any volunteers?"

Tim Purdy, a member of the Chamber of Commerce, whose business was managing farms around the United States from his office in Cabot Cove, said he'd check on Rory, and left the hall.

"You can always count on Tim," said Seth, sitting down.

The meeting lasted another half hour. Although there was disagreement on a number of issues, it warmed my heart to see how the citizens of the town could come together and negotiate their differences.

After, coffee, tea, juice, and doughnuts were served at the rear of the hall. I enjoyed apple juice and a cinnamon doughnut with friends, many of whom expressed pleasure that I would be in town for the festivities.

"I was wondering whether you would do a Christmas reading for the kids this year, Jessica," Cynthia Curtis, director of our library and a member of the town board, said.

"I'd love to," I replied. "Some Christmas stories? Fables?"

"Whatever you choose to do," she said.

But then I thought of Seth, who was chatting in a far corner with our sheriff and another good friend, Morton Metzger. "Seth usually does the reading, doesn't he?" I said.

"Oh, I don't think he'd mind deferring to you this year, Jess. It would be a special treat for the kids to have a famous published author read Christmas stories to them."

I suppose my face expressed concern about usurping Seth.

"Why don't you do the reading together?" Cynthia suggested. "That would be a different approach."

I liked that idea, and said so. "I'll discuss it with Seth as soon as we leave," I said.

Seth and Mort approached me.

"Feel like an early lunch?" Seth asked.

"Sure. Nice presentation, Mort," I said, referring to the talk he'd given about how the police department would maintain order during the festival.

"Been doing it long enough," he said. "Ought to know what's needed. 'Course, never have to worry about anybody gettin' too much out of hand. Folks really pick up on the Christmas spirit around here— love thy neighbor, that sort of thing."

We decided to have lunch at Mara's Luncheonette, down by the water and a favorite local hangout. The weather was cold and nasty; snow was forecast for the evening.

"I hope Mara made up some of her clam chowder," I said as the three of us prepared to leave the hall. "Chowder and freshly baked bread is really appealing."

We reached the door and were in the process of putting on our coats when Tim Purdy entered. I knew immediately from the expression on his face that something was wrong. He came directly to Sheriff Metzger and said something to him Seth and I couldn't hear. Mort's face turned serious, too.

"What's wrong?" I asked.

"There's been an accident out at Rory's place," Purdy said.

"An accident? To Rory?" Seth asked.

"Afraid so," said Purdy. "Rory is dead!"

"Rory is dead?" Seth and I said in unison.

Purdy nodded grimly.

"Means Santa's dead, too," Seth said.

He was right. My eyes filled as I said, "I'm suddenly not very hungry."

MURDER, SHE WROTE:
Murder on Parade

by Jessica Fletcher & Donald Bain
Based on the Universal television series
Created by Peter S. Fischer,
Richard Levinson & William Link

Every Fourth of July, the town of Cabot Cove
hosts an elaborate celebration—and no one is
more enthusiastic than the town's newest
resident, corporate mogul Joseph Lennon.
He's desperate to give the town an unwanted
21st-century makeover, including financing a
fireworks extravaganza to rival New York City's.

But when Lennon's lifeless body is found
floating in the water outside his office,
Jessica Fletcher has no choice but to investigate
her fellow Cabot Cove citizens to find out if
one of them is capable of murder...

FROM THE MYSTERY SERIES
MURDER,
SHE WROTE
by Jessica Fletcher & Donald Bain

Based on the Universal television series
Created by Peter S. Fischer, Richard Levinson & William Link

Available wherever books are sold or at
penguin.com